I0679044

Blind Woman's Bluff

Michael Paulson

BooksForABuck.com
2014

BLIND WOMAN'S BLUFF Copyright 2014 by Michael Paulson, all rights reserved. No portion of this novel may be duplicated, transmitted, or stored in any form without the express written permission of the publisher.

Warning: The unauthorized reproduction or distribution of this copyrighted work is illegal. Criminal copyright infringement, including infringement without monetary gain, is investigated by the FBI and is punishable by up to 5 years in federal prison and a fine of $250,000.

This is a work of fiction. All characters, events, and locations are fictitious or used fictitiously. Any resemblance to actual events or people is coincidental.

Prologue
"A Doll's Tale"

"**W**here the fuck're my Bling-blings?"

The screaming man was Harry Steiner. He was short, thin, and slightly built with olive-white skin. His skull was enormous, shaped like a slightly flattened volleyball. His black hair was cut in bowl-fashion, the fringes of which hung below a rumpled, aluminum-foil cap.

"Please don't hit me again!"

The plea came from Meri Darling. She was a twenty-something model-type; tall, gaunt, blue-eyed and bottled blonde. The scent of lavender floated around her denim-clad form. It mixed with Meri's fear and sweat, producing a murky, cloying cloud.

"You brought the fuckin' doll in from Paris!" Steiner's voice had a nasal tenor, with mushy overtones due to tooth loss. "That means, Cunt, you still got the fuckin' doll."

"I'm not lying, Harry." Her terror-struck eyes scanned the little man's ugly face. "Sydney's got the doll."

"I'm Captain a' the ship!" Steiner bellowed. His hands went up to the metal Tam O'Shanter and stroked its blinking, colored lights, as if to sooth his anger. "If I say you got the fuckin' doll, you got the fuckin' doll."

With the exception of the blinking foil, the elfin male dressed entirely in black. His leather jacket and shoes were new. His dirty t-shirt bore a leering, gray skull and his jeans were frayed at the cuffs. Holes gaped at the ankles in his socks.

"You're the Captain, Harry," she whimpered.

"I give the orders!"

"You give the orders, Harry. But, I'm telling the truth."

The oddly-matched pair were sprawled on the floor next to a small dining booth in an old Dodge Van. The vehicle idled in a parking space at Logan International Airport. It was mid-October."You should'a stopped Sydney-Boy, Cunt."

"I tried, Harry. I swear to God, I tried."

A frantic struggle had disheveled their clothing. Near the vehicle's rear door was Meri's handbag, its contents turned out. Closer to the couple was a pair of round sunglasses with silver frames: Steiner's spectacles.

"You didn't try hard enough!" the elfin man returned.

"There was nothing I could do. Sydney had a gun."

A bleeding split disfigured the young woman's lower lip. Bruised tissue nearly closed her left eye. Her Grecian nose and delicate chin were swollen and smeared with blood.

"Nobody in my organization gets guns but me! That's my number one rule."

"No, Harry. That's rule number three."

Steiner weighed Meri's words. In so doing, his forehead bulged like an overinflated inner tube, pulsing with pressure. Seconds passed. Then he asked if she was certain of her facts.

"Positive," Meri returned, her voice box quivering beneath his thumbs. "Rule number one bans pineapple from pizza."

"What's rule four?"

"No mixing vodka with prune juice."

He squinted in confusion, his lips forming a kiss-like pucker beneath his long, crooked nose. "Rule number two?"

"No discussing your genitalia size during sex."

"That one I remember." Abruptly, Steiner shot out a hand and gripped Meri's throat. "But none of 'em gets me the doll."

Her long fingers wrapped around his boyish wrist, trying to ease the pressure on her larynx. "I can help you get it back, Harry."

"You?" he scoffed. "You gave the doll to Sydney-Boy in the first place."

"Harry, listen to me. Nikolay Kandinsky will be back in town in less than a month. You know what he'll do if you don't hand over the doll."

"Of course I know!" Steiner winced. "Kandinsky'll chew me a new asshole. Then the bastard'll shove in a bridge-piling." The little man let go a whimper. "I hate when that happens."

"It won't. Not if we get the doll from Sydney."

"Tell that to the splinters in my 'roids." The corners of Steiner's mouth quivered. "How big's Sydney-boy's gun?"

"Real big."

"Bigger than mine?"

Meri's chin moved slightly within the confines of his grasp.

"How much bigger?" he asked, his voice harsh, demanding.

"Deep breaths, Harry."

"Is it a lot bigger?"

"Size doesn't matter, Harry. Everybody says that size doesn't matter."

Steiner abruptly released his grip, and eased onto his haunches; his eyeballs rolling back into his head. Meri's fingers went to her throat and massaged the fresh bruises. The moldy smell of him lingered over her like rotting death.

"I gotta' know, Meri. You gotta' tell me. No bullshit." Steiner held one arm out and slowly spread the fingers of that hand, eyeing the digits as if having never seen them before. "What about the other—you know?"

Meri Darling hesitated. A lie, considering Steiner's agitated state, could be fatal. The truth could also get her killed. Then an idea struck. It still tempted fate. However an oblique falsehood might tilt the odds of survival in her favor.

"It's even bigger than Leon's, Harry."

The little man stood up; his small chest heaving, the foil cap just touching the van's ceiling. Despite his diminutive stature, Steiner loomed above Meri like a stubby ogre. Suddenly, he turned and eyed the emptiness at the rear of the van, as if noticing something or someone.

"Did you show her your dick, Leon?" the little man growled to the empty space.

"He forced me to look at it, Harry." Meri Darling quickly shifted into a sitting position, the corners of her mouth quivering as she fought to keep her lips from spreading into a mocking smile. "I didn't want to." She slowly skidded away from him. "I tried to avert my eyes. But Leon wouldn't let me. He kept saying how much bigger his was than yours."

"I should cut off your balls, Leon! I should shove 'em down your throat!"

To those who had not experienced Harry Steiner's schizophrenic outbursts, his invisible tormenter, Leon, was a source of amusement. For Meri, Leon was a means of taunting Steiner. But as far as the little man was concerned, Leon was all too real. They were inexorably linked for eternity like the two venom shooting heads on the serpent Amphisbaena.

"Leon shook it at me, Harry." She paused a beat, enjoying the impact her lies had on Steiner's interaction with his schizophrenic hallucination. "Once he got the wrinkles out, it looked like a purple-headed snake. All I could think of was you, and how it could spit venom in my eye."

The little man staggered toward the rear of the van, his legs splayed, his narrow shoulders bunched. "I'm gonna' kill you, Leon!" His jug-ears flushed crimson with rage. "I'm gonna' kill you so dead you'll be dead a thousand years before you're dead!"

A siren sounded in the distance. Steiner abruptly stopped and twisted toward the noise, as if trying to gauge its distance.

"What's the matter, Harry? Did Leon bad-mouth you, again?"

Steiner faced the rear of the van, again. For many seconds he stood in silence as if listening. Then the little man twisted toward the blonde, his mouth slightly open in surprise.

"Leon says he's gonna' piss on my grave."

"That is so like him, Harry."

"He says that Sydney-Boy knows 'bout the Bling-blings."

Meri Darling cringed with renewed fear. "That's because Leon told him."

Once more Steiner faced the rear of the van, again glaring at the emptiness. "You been jaw-flappin', Leon?"

"Leon wants the doll for himself, Harry. He helped Sydney take it, from me." Sadistic crinkles formed at the corners of her eyes as her courage regrouped. "Then Leon tried to rape me."

"You bastard, Leon!" Suddenly, both of Steiner's hands pawed at the foil, repeatedly forming it across his skull. "My head is killing me."

"It's Leon, Harry."

"No. The feds are brain-draining me, again."

"Only because Leon told them to, Harry. I heard him. He and the feds are in it, together." She wetted her lips. "They're after your brilliance, your talent, your charisma."

"They've gone lower. Sweet Jesus! They got me by the balls!"

"Try your mantra, Harry. Like your P-Doc told you."

The little man twisted toward her, the ugliness in his face accented by lines of despair. "Leon's got the feds suckin' me dry and you're talkin' mantra?"

"You're right, Harry." Meri quickly got to her feet, crouching slightly beneath the van's ceiling. "When you're right, you're right. And you're right."

"About what, for the love of God? My scrotum's shriveling."

"Leon. But, don't worry. All we have to do is outsmart him."

"Nobody outsmarts Leon. Nobody."

"Together, we can."

He pressed the heels of his hands to his eyes. "I can't think when the feds are wringing my balls!"

"Let me do the thinking, Harry."

"My whole body's frying!" His mitts moved to the nape of his neck, clawing at it. "I'll tear you apart, Leon. I'm gonna' shove a wrecking ball up your ass and shake it 'til your eyes bug out!"

"Listen to me, Harry. Mike Zeeman and Tio Menotti will be out on parole soon. You remember me telling you?"

The pain eased and the little man's hands dropped to his sides. Steiner's face, wet with perspiration, softened slightly.

"Tio and 'Baby'." He took a handkerchief from his trouser pocket and wiped at the moisture dribbling across his cheeks. "So what?"

"They'll help us, Harry."

"Why would they?"

"They're in love with me. They'll do anything I say."

Steiner squinted at her suspiciously. "You said they were gonna' kill you 'cause you rolled over on 'em."

"Don't worry about that, Harry. I can fix it."

"Fix or not, they got no reason to help me."

"They'll do it if I ask."

"I ain't so sure. For some reason people don't like me, once they get to know me."

"Baby and Tio will need money. We'll pay them. People always like you after they get paid."

The elfin man wagged his head, the foil cap sliding back and forth with the movement. "Forget it."

"Baby's nobody to mess with, Harry. Neither is Tio."

"I heard they're tough. I know they're also on Boston P.D.'s radar." His head made another negative move. "I don't need their shit comin' back to bite me." He winced, his knees tilting together. "I got enough aggravation in my fun parts."

"You want the doll, don't you?"

"Yeah."

"Without Baby and Tio we can't get it." Meri Darling tilted toward the little man. "In November, Sydney's taking his wife to Hull."

"Not if he's deader than dead—like I'm gonna' make him."

"You can't kill Sydney, Harry. Not 'til we get the doll. And that's going to happen in Hull." She made a casual movement with one hand. "After that, we'll have Baby and Tio take care of Sydney. They're good at that, Harry. They know how to cover their tracks."

"No way. Sydney-Boy's my meat."

"We can't take a chance with Kandinsky, Harry. If you do the killing, the Russian might ask questions. We don't want Kandinsky asking questions, Harry."

"But, Sydney-Boy's gotta' pay!"

"He will, Harry. I'll tell Baby and Tio to take special care of him, just for you."

The little man thrust a finger at her. "Okay. But, I get to watch."

"Sure, Harry. We'll go to Hull and get front row seats."

"What makes you think Sydney-Boy'll bring the doll there?"

"Sydney takes the doll every place he goes."

"Yeah. Every place."

"You and me and Baby and Tio will go to Hull. We'll wait for Sydney and wifey. When they get there, I'll have Baby and Tio make their move. You and me will sit back and enjoy the show. Okay, Harry?"

"I don't get it."

"Get what?"

"Why're them two ain't gonna' make their move until we're in Hull? Why not Boston? I know my way around, Boston. If things go south, in Boston I know where to hole up. I don't know shit from Shinola in Hull."

"Hull's a small town, Harry. It has a small police force. They won't know how to handle a killing. But, best of all, you and me and Baby and Tio aren't known there. When Sydney turns up dead and nobody can link it to you. That's the important thing, Harry. No matter what, we've have to protect you. You're the important one. You're the one with the brains."

The little man considered the scenario she had laid out for many seconds. Then, his head did another back and forth spin.

"What if your pals run off with the doll?" Steiner demanded.

"They won't, Harry. Not with you and me there to make sure they don't."

"Says you."

"Leon got us into this, Harry." Meri Darling forced a nervous smile. "Like it or not, Baby and Tio are our only chance at getting straight with Kandinsky."

Again, Steiner weighed her words. Again, he gave his head a wag.

"Why not?" she asked.

"Them two are still in the joint. You said so, yourself. And like you pointed out, Kandinsky'll be back in Boston within a month. We gotta' come up with something, now."

"Baby and Tio will be out in two weeks, Harry. Relax. We'll have plenty of time before Kandinsky returns."

There was more silence. Then Steiner turned to refocus his eyes on the back of the van. He cocked his head several times as if listening to someone speaking softly. Afterward, the little man faced the beautiful blonde.

"Nietzsche said, 'The lie is a condition of life.'" The little man's eyes narrowed on Meri, his mouth twisting into an icy smile. "That means lies end with death." Abruptly, Steiner's face stiffened. "You get my meaning, Cunt?"

She shivered with fear. "I'm not lying, Harry."

"Tomorrow, you call Baby and Tio at the joint where they're hangin'. Tomorrow, you tell 'em you wanna' meet at Derne Street, 5 B—Sydney-Boy's flop—soon's they're out." The lid on Steiner's left eye drooped, slightly. "Tell 'em you got two grand to spread around. And Meri…" He paused, gritting his teeth. "You'd better not be playin' me." He jabbed a finger at her. "Or, I'll add your pretty blues to my pickled peeper's collection."

The blonde nodded, still shivering under his glare. Meri knew that Steiner would make good on his threat. Steiner always made good on his threats.

"I'll handle it, Harry."

"We're leavin'." He pointed at the van's steering wheel.

"What about my car?"

"It stays."

"But…"

"Move, Cunt!"

Meri scrambled into the driver's seat. "Where to?"

"Sydney-Boy's place." Steiner's bloated forehead flexed like melting gelatin. "I'll show him whose fuckin' gun is bigger."

"But Tio and Baby…"

"They're Plan 'C'," he cut in, impatiently.

Meri Darling frowned, her face showing bewilderment. "What's Plan 'B'?"

"Still workin' Plan 'B.'" Steiner went over to his sunglasses, picked them up and slipped them on. "Plan 'B's the thorny one. Gotta' be real careful workin' Plan 'B.' One mistake with Plan 'B' and you'll find your dick in a vice. And take it from me, you don't want your dick in a vice." He moved to the front of the van and slumped into the passenger seat. "Drive."

Meri Darling shifted uneasily in the seat, carefully considering the little man's body language. He was tilted forward, slightly; eying her askance. His chin was tucked, a cruel smile curling the corners of his lips. Meri had seen that look on the little man's face before. It was the last look he gave another woman who had crossed him. She was dead, her eyes now part of Harry's private collection.

"You can count on me, Harry." Her left hand slipped down to the door handle. Her fingers curled around it. "You know that, don't you?"

"Sure, I know." He offered her a plastic grin. "I see the blood in your eyes."

A moment later, the driver's door banged opened and Meri Darling leaped out. She broke into a frantic run. A run for her life.

"I'll kill you, Bitch!" Harry Steiner clamored from the van. "I'm gonna' kill you so dead, you'll be deader than dead, before you're even dead!" He stamped one foot. "Now, you made my head hurt, again."

Chapter 1
"Wrong Apartment"

"Three years in the joint and nothin'."

The speaker, Tio Menotti, was short, burly, bald and pushing fifty. He moved like a bulldog, and had a face to match. But, his voice was high and sharp, like a terrier's yip.

"Out two days," he continued, "suddenly Meri's gotta' see us? I don't like it."

The burly man wore a wrinkled brown suit and a black overcoat. His white shirt was yellowed around the collar, its frayed cuffs jutted below his coat-arms. Menotti's big feet were encased in scuffed black leather; the soles worn-down.

"Two days isn't sudden." Mike Zeeman had a pleasingly deep voice, with a Boston accent.

"Baby, I'm tellin' ya two days' notice after three years is something to worry about."

"Paranoia has you by the short hairs, Tio."

Zeeman was fortyish, his heavily muscled body wedge-shaped. His hair was coarse, dark, and wavy; parted in the middle. The tall man had a Greek nose, and a firm wide mouth which, at the moment, was compressed in a thin cruel line. His eyes were intensely dark, as if molten with fury. Men found Zeeman intimidating. Women found him irresistible.

"Where Meri Darling's involved, Baby, my short and curlies have a right to be scared." Menotti held out a thick, wide palm; his face crimson from the cold. "You and me did three years on account of her."

"Old news, Tio."

The two men were moving quickly, following the sidewalk fronting Derne Street, their cleated heels clicking in unison. It was a cold, gray afternoon in early November.

"She screws us over and then wants to meet?" the burly man ranted. "That's a lot of balls, if you ask me."

"Nobody's asking."

Zeeman wore khaki slacks, western boots, a plaid shirt, and a flight jacket. With each determined stride, he exuded the impression of a man on a grim mission.

"Like she didn't think we meant it when we said we'd kill her?" said Menotti.

"You're going to blow a gasket."

"Baby, I'm gonna' blow a gasket 'cause I'm wondering how she plans to screw us." The burly man jabbed a stubby forefinger from one hand into the palm of the other. "I'll give you any odds you want this whole gig is a setup."

"Maybe."

"No maybe about it, Baby."

The tall man glanced over at his partner, grinning. "We won't know 'til we talk to Meri."

"I ain't talking to her. You wanna talk to Meri, fine." Menotti fanned the air in front of him. "But I ain't talking to her." The burly man hesitated for two breaths. Then he said, "That note didn't look like her handwriting."

"It wasn't."

"Then how come you think she sent it?"

Zeeman shoved his big hands deep into his jacket pockets, to protect them from the chilly wind. "I don't."

"Then why're we out here freezing our jewels?"

"Nobody forced you to come."

The change from sunshine brought a granite sky and gusting winds. The frosty air carried the promise of snow. Darkness would arrive by half-five.

"What's Meri's address?" Menotti tugged at his red nose, glancing at the building numbers.

"I told you."

"I forget."

"Derne Street, 5-B."

The burly man cleared his throat. "B?" he muttered eventually. "That's basement, ain't it?"

"We'll know when we get there."

Zeeman's tone was irritated. Nevertheless, the importance of Menotti's observation had not eluded him. Meri Darling was the penthouse type. Basements had never been part of her varied and deeply illicit lifestyle.

"Baby, I ain't never gonna' forgive her for rolling over on us at trial."

"You think I'm happy about it?" Zeeman's face twitched as sudden anger sent the right side of his mouth down slightly.

"I'm just sayin' it's crazy to re-hook with Meri Darling when we know a re-hook'll get us screwed."

"We need the money, Tio."

Menotti pulled a thin, green-dappled, cigar from his coat and stuffed it into his mouth. "I was running a *superfecta* when Meri's testimony booted us behind bars." His tongue lolled the tobacco stick back and forth until it lodged in one corner, angled toward the grim sky. "My brother-in-law collected the winnings. Never saw a damn dime." His jaw muscles rippled. "I woulda' killed the son-of-a-bitch, but for my sister." The burly man nodded his bald head, slightly. "I might, anyway."

"What's past is past."

"That's what you're gonna' tell the cops when she gets us busted?"

Zeeman nodded, but he was paying little attention to Menotti's words. The tall man's mind was on his own emotions. He could verbally dismiss Meri's betrayal. But his heart and soul had other ideas. Zeeman knew that if he lost control, he would kill her.

"Baby, you know how much I'll get from Social Security when I retire?"

The burly man took out a disposable lighter and flicked it to life. He touched the orange flame to the cigar's end and puffed until the smoldering tip took on an even cherry color.

"What has that to do with anything, Tio?"

"I won't be able to buy paper to wipe my ass." The burly man put the lighter back into his pocket. "Because of Meri, my retirement's gonna' be sticky."

"That's an image I didn't need."

The minutes ticked by.

"Baby, since when did Meri have two grand?"

"We won't know 'til we see her."

They continued for another block.

"Baby, I say we kill Meri."

"Yeah, Tio, we're out here, walking all this way, freezing our balls, so we can kill her."

Zeeman was tired and cold. The muscles in his legs and shoulders twitched with adrenalin. The closer they got to Meri's address, the angrier he became.

"We talked about it," the burly man pressed. "We both talked about killin' her."

"Talk is cheap."

"Cheap, my ass. It's all we talked about for three years." He paused to take in a deep breath. "I was looking forward to it."

"So deal with the disappointment." Zeeman's voice betrayed his growing agitation.

"It's just that you know how you get, when you get how you get."

"I won't get how I get."

Menotti's eyebrows arched, as he eyed his partner. "But, we're gonna' kill her?"

"Someday, Tio. Not today."

The burly man puffed on the cigar for nearly a minute, and then said, "Baby, I've been doing a rethink."

"You're always doing a rethink."

"I'm thinking we give Meri a chance." The burly man took the cigar from his mouth and flicked a finger across the smoldering end, to dislodge the ash. "You know, a little breathing room so she can explain."

Zeeman smirked. "You want her to explain before we kill her?"

"Baby, I'm just saying Meri could have reasons for doing us dirt."

"People always have reasons, Tio."

"You know what I mean." Menotti glanced at his partner from the corners of his eyes. "Then there's the money."

"The two grand she offered?"

"We could use that two grand."

"Yeah, Tio. It'll give us two grand more than we've got."

"All's I'm sayin' is, maybe we should forgive and forget."

"After we get the two grand?"

"Well, that goes without saying."

Zeeman's laughed softly. "Tio, you'd kiss Meri's ass."

"Yeah, Baby, like you haven't?"

An orange corvette, with the top down, rumbled past. Driving it was an elderly man wearing a ski cap, parka, and gloves. He was hunched over the steering wheel. His face looked purple with cold. Beside him was a young blonde draped in furs, and jewelry.

"That's what I need," declared Menotti, pointing after the car.

"You couldn't afford the tire stems."

"Not the car. The old guy's parka." The burly man slapped his hands together to generate heat, as they continued along the sidewalk. "Did you see the fur on his hood? Probably wolf."

"What've you got against wolves?"

"Nothing. But without hair my head's got no insulation." Menotti hunched his shoulders, against the wind. "I think my brain's icing up."

"Maybe that'll do it some good."

Menotti moistened his lips, hesitated. "Once we collect that two grand, I'm gettin' that parka." He glanced up at the gray sky. "That's why I've always hated bein' a plumber."

"You hate plumbing because you can't wear a parka covered in dead wolf?"

"I hated it because every job dumped me dick-deep in ice water. Talk about shrinkage."

"You should've become an electrician, like me."

"I couldn't. After you and me got busted that first time, they dumped me in Old Colony Correctional. It was learn plumbing or hair design." He shivered. "When you're fourteen and locked up with a bunch of rough, tattooed bastards who'd gut you for a quarter, you don't learn hair design." Menotti took a couple of puffs on the cigar, his eyes resuming their tour of the neighborhood. "You were lucky. You got sent to Pondville."

"Yeah, Tio, I did a cakewalk all the way to my eighteenth birthday."

"All's I'm sayin' is, Pondville had a more liberal view of rehabilitating youthful offenders."

The two men traversed another block.

"I wonder what Meri's been up to?" Menotti said. He waved the smoldering tobacco-stub at a trio of tired buildings. "Or, maybe I should say 'down to'?"

"Don't be quick to judge," Zeeman returned. "Those townhouses cost a fortune."

Road traffic accompanied them for another two blocks.

"Baby, we gonna' take the job?"

"We got seven bucks between us, Tio," Zeeman replied, without enthusiasm. "Meri's offering two grand. What do you think?"

"I'm thinking we take the job." The burly man puffed several times on the shrinking cigar. Then his voice became concerned. "Only we don't know what the job is."

"Meri'll tell us."

They crossed a street against the light.

"Baby, it just hit me."

"Birds are flying south, Tio. Shit falls."

"Not that. I'm wondering how Meri got two grand."

"Do you care?"

Menotti gave his partner a penetrating look under lowered brows. "Not so long as it don't land us back in the joint."

"You're a man of rare scruples, Tio."

"Well, that goes without saying." The burly man gave his bald head a thoughtful nod. "Maybe Meri won it at the track?"

"Horses don't run in winter, Tio."

"I'm thinking last summer."

"Since when did Meri save money?"

Menotti screwed up his bulldog face. "Maybe she's got a rich boyfriend?"

"Maybe."

"Or maybe she had a rich boyfriend. Only, she killed him."

"For a lousy two grand?"

"I'm just sayin' there could be lots of reasons how Meri got the money. Some not so nice."

There was another period of street noise.

"I dreamed about Meri, while we were in the joint." Menotti chewed the remains of the cigar. "Bet you did, too." Then, he took the butt from his mouth and gave it a toss. "You think Meri dreamed 'bout us?"

"Everybody has nightmares."

Zeeman stopped in front of a dilapidated row-house. Its brown brick went three-stories high with white sandstone trim. The wooden front door, up five steps from the sidewalk, was a round-headed double leaf with arched panels. Flanking it were vaulted windows with painted flower boxes mounted to the sills. Above the door was a brass plaque bearing the number: '5'. Another door, three steps down from the sidewalk, was wood and round-topped. This marked the entrance to the building's basement level.

"This is it, Tio."

The burly man walked past, stopped and looked back, eyeing the old building skeptically. "It's a dump."

Zeeman pointed at the plaque. "Numbers don't lie."

"So much for buyin' a parka."

A teenage girl came out of the upper entrance. She hurried down the steps, holding a lit cigarette. Tio Menotti eyed the weed-stick with despair. She gave the two men a quick visual once-over, and then hurried on.

"Baby, you think that kid's mother knows she smokes?"

"Not our business, Tio."

"All's I'm saying is a kid that age shouldn't smoke. It's bad for her hormones."

"Let's let the kid's mother worry about hormones while you and me talk to Meri."

"Forget Meri." Menotti clapped his hands over his ears, trying to warm them. "Let's get our summer clothes out of storage. Then, we'll jump a freight to California. I got contacts there."

"We got contacts here."

"But, in California we can start fresh."

"For guys like us, there are no fresh starts." Zeeman headed for the lower-level steps.

"Ain't goin' in, Baby," Menotti called to his partner's back. "If Meri's living there, ain't no money so there's no point in goin' in."

Zeeman's shrugged, his lips thinning. Then he went down the steps to the basement door. He tried the knob. It turned. The tall man pushed and the door creaked open. Ahead of him another short series of steps descended into a tomblike corridor. He followed the stairs down.

"Cozy, huh?" Menotti said, clamoring after his partner.

"Like the path to Dracula's love-nest."

"Baby, maybe you should go first."

"I thought you weren't going in."

"Why wouldn't I go in? Of course I'm goin' in."

Zeeman led the way along the corridor, with Menotti following. Their heels clicked out echoes on the concrete. Overhead two bare bulbs, dangling about fifteen feet apart, splashed yellow on the floor.

A scrap of paper was thumb-nailed below the brass 'B' on one of the three doors. A second had a hand-painted 'exit' sign, above it. Zeeman went over to the 'exit door' and pulled it open. This gave him a view of a large yard thick with tall weeds and grass. He shut it and went over to the third door. Upon opening it, he saw a shadowy staircase leading up.

"No heat." Menotti shivered. He glanced back the way they had come as if wishing he had not followed. "Must get freezing cold in winter."

"Probably why it's freezing, now."

"Baby, you think I should ask for what Meri owes me?"

"Did asking do any good, before?"

"Not so far."

"Then, why bother?" Zeeman went to the door labelled with the 'B', and tore the paper free.

"What is it?"

"Note. Computer printed." Zeeman handed the correspondence to his partner.

The burly man glanced at it. "We come all this way and she ain't in?" He crumpled the paper and dropped it to the floor. "That means there won't be any ass-grab."

Zeeman eyed his partner in bewilderment. "Ass-grab?"

"It's our thing, Baby."

"I've known you thirty-five years, Tio. Not once did I grab your ass."

"Meri and me."

There was a short pause while Zeeman considered the other man's words. "Tio, since when did Meri grab your ass?"

"Baby, I grabbed hers."

Zeeman opened the apartment door, and peered inside. "Something's not right."

"Meri never complained."

"I'm talking about this setup."

"I knew that from the git-go. But you didn't listen."

The tall man's eyes went from wall to wall, ceiling to floor. Directly ahead, painted wooden shelves were lined with dozens of dusty books cloaked in colorful wrappers. From the ceiling dangled glass fixtures in the shape of mushrooms. At room-center sat a heavy couch with wooden disks for legs, and a covering of maroon velveteen.

"Is this what they call, shabby chic?" Menotti asked, peeking around his partner.

"In our day it was called a slum."

Zeeman stepped onto a landing above a single flight of stairs. These descended to the apartment's front room.

"Meri?" he called.

"What're you yellin' for?" Menotti complained, rubbernecking at the gloomy interior. "The note said she ain't here. You think all that stuff is antiques?"

"Yeah. And I'm the king of Boston Commons."

To Zeeman's left was a kitchen-dining area. Computer printers cluttered the dining portion of the space. Several large computer-monitors stood on a Masonite counter. Near them were a computer keyboard, a printer and a stack of external hard drives.

Across from this, within the kitchen proper, an aged refrigerator rattled between a wall and another counter inset with a sink and its drip pan. To his right, Zeeman noted a hallway that led to the rest of the apartment.

"Meri used to be classy," Menotti grunted. He went to the landing rail, still rubbernecking. "What d'you think happened?"

"Poverty. Just hang loose."

Zeeman descended the steps, uneasiness showing in his handsome face.

"We get paid up front, Baby," Menotti called. He heeled the door shut and followed. "Cash. And I'm counting it before we turn a cog." The burly man stopped at the stair-bottom, watching his partner. "Are you listening, Mike?"

In the front room Zeeman pointed to the computer hardware. "Meri must be living with a geek."

"Them guy's is a dime a dozen."

"Yeah," Zeeman returned, his voice caustic with sarcasm. "Living with me was upscale."

"You gotta' quit putting yourself down, Baby." Menotti ran his stubby fingers across his bare scalp, grinning ruefully. "We got plenty of style, when we put it on."

"Jailbirds with style?" The tall man's words were heavy with sarcasm. "You've always had a way with words, Tio."

"Baby, you know what I mean."

"From the looks of this flop, the geek doesn't earn much," Zeeman remarked. "So what's the draw for Meri?"

"It's the economy. You heard me talk about the economy." The burly man sucked his teeth. "It's got everybody by the balls."

"Not everybody."

"Well, it's got you and me by the balls."

"Life, in general, has you and me by the balls."

Menotti frowned, his eyes again moving about the place. "We gonna' wait?"

"I'll check things out. You watch the street."

"Gotcha."

Zeeman headed down the hallway. The burly man strode into the kitchen.

In the bedroom, Zeeman carefully looked around. The space was almost as large as the front room. Its yellow, plastered walls had cobwebs near the ceiling. A door on the south wall accessed a closet. The north wall held a wide window, providing a view of the property's fenced-in back yard. Against the east wall was a Queen Anne style desk with chair, and a four-drawer bureau. Occupying the west wall was a king-size bed. A fuzzy, brown carpet covered the floor.

His eyes locked upon the framed photograph atop the bureau. It was of a thirtyish couple he had never seen. The man was blond, well-muscled and tanned. The woman was dark-haired, pale and beautiful. Both were smiling. From their clothing and the bouquet, it was a wedding portrait.

Zeeman quickly opened the bureau's drawers. Then he searched each, closing the drawer as he finished.

The third drawer had a false bottom. Within the secret space were half a dozen snapshots of a nude woman he recognized as Meri Darling. There were several more pictures. These were European shots of Meri and the man in the wedding photo. Zeeman tucked the pictures into his pocket. Then he closed the bureau and went over to the closet. He tugged on the door but it didn't budge, its knob fitted with a lock. Zeeman slid his fingers along the top of the doorframe searching for a key. He found nothing.

Menotti looked over one shoulder as he heard his partner's rapidly returning footsteps.

"Smorgasbord, Baby." The burly man stood at the counter next to the refrigerator, building a cold-cut sandwich. "Step up and grab the lunch we skipped."

"No time to eat, Tio."

"Baby, the fridge is loaded with goodies. Sliced meat. Four kinds of cheese. One of 'em's *bier kase*, my favorite."

Zeeman's face showed marked anxiety. "I said it's no time to eat."

"But, I'm hungry." The burly man took a bite and turned to face his partner. "And you remember how the prison Doc said I gotta' watch my sugar count."

"This isn't Meri's flat."

"Sure it is. You saw the note."

"It's the note that started me wondering."

Menotti took another bite and chewed out, "Wondering what?"

"Since when does Meri know enough about computers to write a note?"

There were seconds of silence as Menotti munched and mulled, his face vacant. Then, abruptly, the burly man swallowed. A split second later his eyes bulged with terrified realization.

"Shit!" Menotti's cry echoed back from the low ceiling. "That lousy bitch!"

"My thoughts, exactly."

"Meri set us up!" Menotti stuffed the sandwich into his coat, and hurried toward the staircase. "I'm gonna' kill her, Baby! I don't care what you say, I'm gonna' kill her."

Zeeman fell in behind his partner, as both men hurried up the steps. "So much for forgive and forget."

"We shouldn't have come in," Menotti seethed. "You heard me, Baby. I told you, we shouldn't go in."

"I heard."

Before either man reached the knob, the apartment door swung inward.

"Jesus!" Menotti squealed, jumping back in shock.

Chapter 2
"Unpleasant Surprises"

Harry Steiner stood in the doorway. The little man was dressed in the same clothing he'd worn during his interaction with Meri Darling weeks before, including the sunglasses and foil headgear. But, the lights on his makeshift cap no longer worked.

"You want something?" Zeeman growled.

"This and that, Mr. Zeeman," the little man replied. Steiner's mouth curled up at the corners in a self-satisfied manner. "The other thing, too."

Zeeman's right hand went into his jacket pocket; the fingers coiling around a revolver secreted there. He eyed the little man malevolently, not unlike a python considering the snack-potential of a rabbit.

Steiner stepped onto the landing. "How's tricks, Menotti?" He went past the two men, quickly clattering down the staircase.

"You know him?" Zeeman asked, glancing at his partner.

Menotti shook his head. "Never seen the creep, before." Then he called after Steiner: "Does your headgear come with stereo?"

Steiner stopped at the foot of the staircase, and looked up at the other two. "Protection."

"Where I come from safe sex starts farther down."

"The CIA's on my fuckin' ass, Menotti!" Steiner's head rocked back and forth atop his neck, as if having heard something unnerving but unable to pinpoint the sound. "They know I'm a genius. They're after my plans. They're trying to suck me dry."

"You hear that, Baby? The genius is being sucked dry."

Zeeman grinned. "Yippee-ki-yi-yea, Tio."

"Glad ya made it," the little man said.

Zeeman brushed past his partner, taking the steps down in measured movements, his hand still gripping the gun. At the bottom of the steps, he crowded Steiner.

"You wrote the note, Bad man?"

"Somebody had to, Mr. Zeeman."

"What name's on your dog collar?"

Harry Steiner man retreated from the tall man, like a chicken fleeing a fox. Over one shoulder he identified himself.

"The Mars Steiners?" Menotti mocked, closing the apartment door. "The ones who own all that red sand, up there?"

Steiner frowned, as if seriously considering possibilities, his eyes going to the burly man. After a few seconds, he slowly shook his head.

"My people don't do air-travel, Menotti."

The burly man winked at his partner. "Must be I'm thinking of the Steiners from Poughkeepsie."

"Why would the CIA be interested in you, Bad Man?" Zeeman followed the elfin man.

"Yeah, Creep," chimed Menotti, as he walked down the stairs. "If you're a spy, this country's in deep shit."

"I'm not a spy, Menotti. The Fed's got a brain-drain machine." Steiner stopped his retreat and adjusted the lay of his cap. "They want my juices."

"We must be in more desperate times than I imagined."

"It's Top Secret." One of Steiner's fingers stroked the unlit cap as he put more space between himself and Zeeman. "My battery's dead."

"That would've been my second guess."

"Where's Meri, Bad Man?" Zeeman asked.

"Busy."

"Busy at what?" Menotti demanded.

Steiner shrugged, eying the other two askance. "Just busy."

"I want to see her," Zeeman insisted.

"And Meri's hot to see you, Mr. Zeeman." The little man adjusted his dark glasses. "Meri gave me the lowdown on you guys." Steiner moved his narrow shoulders in a disappointed heave. "Have to tell you. Not what I expected."

"Then we're all surprised."

"You the new boyfriend, Creep?"

"Jealous 'cause you couldn't get into Meri's pants, Menotti?"

The burly man let go a growl and started toward Steiner.

Zeeman cut off his partner's attack by stepping between the two men.

"You don't look like a computer-geek, Bad Man," Zeeman remarked.

Steiner tossed a disinterested glance at the machine on the kitchen counter. "Sydney-Boy's."

"What's a Sydney-Boy?"

"Sydney Popovitch."

"Like pullin' teeth, huh, Baby?" Then the burly man glared at Steiner. "Fill us in on Sydney-Boy, Creep."

"Sydney-Boy's a fuckin' jerk-off, Menotti. All flash. No substance."

"Details, Bad-Man."

"You know what Meri's like, Mr. Zeeman. Always fallin' for shallow types." The little man did a quick, nervous swallow. "No offense intended."

The burly man lit a cigar and blew smoke at Steiner.

"Meri didn't mention you, Bad Man," Zeeman remarked.

"Which gives us pause for reflection, Creep."

"Relax, gentlemen." The little man tapped his left temple. "Nothin' to worry 'bout. Meri and I have known each other for years."

Zeeman's face was hard as flint. "I never worry." His left hand knotted, his shoulder muscles flexed, his entire body tensed for a quick, crushing blow.

"That's gospel, Creep," Menotti chimed. "Baby knows how to take care of anybody who might get worrisome." He grinned. "You feel like a winter dip in the Charles?"

Steiner backpedaled a step, his tongue wetting his lips repeatedly. From the greenish hue spreading across his skin, the little man realized that he was in more trouble than he could handle.

"Meri knows how we operate, Bad-Man. Her not telling about you breaks protocol."

"Yeah, Creep," Menotti added, flanking Steiner. "Meri knows we got protocol up the ying-yang."

"What're you holding back, Bad Man?"

"Shit can come up fast and furious, Mr. Zeeman." Steiner hurried over to the rattan rocker, across from the davenport, and sat down. "When it does, there are complications. In this case, big complications. Complications sometimes ignore protocol."

"What do you think, Tio?"

"I don't like him." Menotti eyed the little man with derisive amusement. "'Specially now that I know the Creep's got complications."

"I'm with you, Tio." The tall man's eyes narrowed on Steiner. "What complications, Bad Man?"

"Not to worry, Mr. Zeeman," the little man returned. "Meri's handling it."

"Handling complications doesn't top Meri's credentials, Bad Man."

Steiner splayed his hands. "Can't a woman change?"

"You wanna' hear change, Creep?" the burly man growled. "Try hanging on a wall upstate, 'cause Meri played dip-the-wick with a horny judge."

"Let it go, Tio," Zeeman cooed.

The little man pointed to the davenport. "Let's talk business."

"We're fussy 'bout how we do business." Menotti blew another stream of smoke at Steiner. "We're fussy 'bout who we do business with. In case you ain't figured it out, Creep, we're fussy."

Steiner jumped to his feet. "You fucks want the two grand, or not?"

"What say I kick his balls past his eyebrows, Baby?"

Mike Zeeman held up a warning hand to his partner. "You got the money with you, Bad Man?"

"I got your front money," Steiner returned. "You'll get the rest after the job's done."

"I want it all up front, Creep."

"Let Bad Man talk, Tio."

"For now, sure." Menotti cracked the knuckles on his right hand as he added. "We'll listen. He'll talk. But if the Creep jumps up again, Baby, his balls will be chimin' in his ears."

"Nietzsche said, 'The best weapon against an enemy is another enemy.'" The little man settled back into the rocker, crossed his legs, and pointed to the table in front of the chair. "Hardware."

Menotti snorted, "You, and your pal, Nietzsche, can kiss my 'hardware' ass."

Steiner looked over at the tall man, the little's eyebrows arched as if in pleading. "I'm tryin' to do business, Mr. Zeeman. How 'bout a little help, here?"

Zeeman went over to the rocker and, with a sharp shoe-jab, put the chair into motion. "Let's get down to cases."

"Yeah, Creep. What's the gambit?" Menotti went over and stood next to his partner.

Steiner dropped his feet to the floor, stopping the chair's back and forth motion. "Just out of stir. No job. No money. Meri and I thought you could use some cash in return for a little help."

"Baby, he's playing us."

"Talk or we walk, Bad Man."

"Couple hours of your time, gentlemen."

"Doing what?"

The little man put his hands together at his narrow chest, dropping his elbows to the rocker's arms. "There's this stolen doll. All you have to do is get it back."

"Doll?" Zeeman echoed, in bewilderment.

"We don't play with dolls, Creep."

"A special doll." Steiner's fingers formed a teepee over his belly. "A collector's item. Getting it back is an easy-peasy job for a couple of pros."

"Sound easy to you, Baby?"

Zeeman wagged his head. "Confusing."

"Want me to recharge the Creep's battery with something hard and heavy?"

"Might come to that, Tio."

Steiner put his tongue between his lips, made a raspberry noise, and then pulled the pink protrusion back. "I'm a busy man, gentlemen. In or out?"

The burly man moved past the rocker then Menotti turned, rested a shoulder against the wall adjacent to the chair, and eyed the back of Steiner's foil adorned head.

"You call it, Baby."

"Question, Bad Man. If you're willing to pay two grand to get the doll back, what's it worth?"

"Let's see the hardware, gentlemen." Steiner smiled at Zeeman for a second. "Then we'll get down and dirty."

"I'm clean," Menotti lampooned. He tossed his partner a wink. "You holdin', Baby?"

"Just the lucky piece between my legs."

"Nietzsche said, 'A casual stroll through the lunatic asylum shows that faith does not prove anything.'" Steiner's tone became acidic. "Gentlemen, my faith is unshakable. But, I can't do business unless you get on board."

Menotti flicked the ash from his cigar with a fingernail, without removing the tobacco stick from his mouth. "How're you fixed for deadly, Steiner?"

The little man casually took a stiletto knife from his jacket pocket. He pressed the button on the handle. Instantly, a glinting blade popped out.

"Scary guy," the burly man scorned.

"Strictly for toenails," Steiner returned.

"Long blade for trimmin' toenails, Creep." Menotti tugged at an earlobe, continuing to eye the back of Steiner's head. "Better put your toe-jabber on the table before I get so scared that I take it from you."

"No can do, Menotti."

The burly man took a threatening step toward Steiner. "Why the hell not?"

"Protection."

"You're already protected, remember?"

"Protection against Leon."

"Who's Leon, Bad Man?" Zeeman's voice echoed his alarm.

Steiner folded the blade back into the handle. "You wouldn't like Leon, Mr. Zeeman." The little man returned the knife to his jacket. "Leon's got attitude, and a big gun."

"What do you think, Baby? Should I show this piece of shit real attitude?"

"Feed him the toe-jabber, Tio, pointy end first."

Menotti, grinning, started toward Steiner.

"Not smart, gentlemen."

"On second thought, Tio," Zeeman intervened, "give Bad Man a chance to finish his show and tell."

"Baby, I never have fun."

"Time's coming." Zeeman glared at Steiner. "You got one shot at it, Bad Man. Make it good—like your life's on the line."

"You get the doll from Sydney-Boy and deliver it to me." Steiner nervously glanced over one shoulder at Menotti. "When I get the doll, you get two grand, less front money." He waggled both his hands. "How much simpler does it have to get?"

"Does this Leon own the doll?"

"It's Meri's, Mr. Zeeman."

"And Leon has it?"

"Leon's not involved."

"Then who has it?"

"Sydney-Boy has it because Sydney-Boy stole it." The little man hesitated. "There'll be a bonus, after you get the doll, for terminating Sydney-Boy."

"How much bonus?"

"Five grand."

"What's this doll look like?" Menotti asked.

"Porcelain head," Steiner returned. "Calf-skin body. Twenty-eight inches tall. Made in 1934." He gave Menotti another wary look. "Dressed in a blue gown and black leather shoes. Real hair, red." The little man smiled. "Like I said, a collector's item."

"When did Meri take an interest in dolls, Bad-Man?"

"What's the difference?"

"Meri never mentioned dolls to us, Creep, that's the difference."

"She took up a hobby. You got a problem with hobbies, Menotti?"

"Nope," Menotti returned. "But a doll that size being an interest to Meri, makes me think there must be more to it. Like, maybe, there's something valuable inside."

"Value's purely sentimental, Menotti." The little man leaned back in the chair, his eyes wide; the pupils mere pinpoints. "Do we deal?"

"Still your call, Baby."

"Sentimental or not, Bad Man, if Sydney Popovitch stole it he's not going to just give it up. Is he armed?"

The little man pursed his lips slowly, as though thoughts were turning in his oddly-shaped head. "If he wasn't I wouldn't need you and Menotti, Mr. Zeeman."

"I'm in if you are, Baby."

"All right, Bad Man. Consider us on board."

"Time to discuss front money, Creep," the burly man said. "I'm thinking that five hundred should do us."

Steiner took a rubber banded roll of cash from a pocket and tossed it onto the table. "Meri thought a thousand split might be close to the mark."

Menotti lunged around the little man and snatched up the bundle.

"Since when did Meri get generous?" Zeeman asked.

"'Is man one of God's blunders or is God one of man's blunders?'" Steiner made an irritating clucking noise with his tongue. "We're suckin' hind tit on this gig, gentlemen, due to a Russian's pending arrival. Are we also in agreement that tomorrow is start day?"

"It's straight, Baby." The burly man handed half the money to his partner. "We eat Italian, tonight."

Zeeman pocketed his portion of the cash. "Why not tonight?"

"I have information that puts Sydney-Boy in Hull, as of tomorrow. Meri thinks it would be best if we take our action there."

"Hull is fine."

"How did Popovitch steal the doll, Creep? Meri's no pushover."

"Sydney-Boy had some help from Leon. Leon's got a real big gun."

"You said Leon wasn't part of this."

"He's not. All you'll have to deal with is Sydney-Boy."

Menotti's face became suspicious. "Baby, I'm not sure two grand is enough if we have to deal with both them guys. Things could get crowded."

"I thought you were tough, Menotti," the little man taunted.

"I am. I just like to know what I'm getting' into. You're sure that Leon clown won't be involved?"

"I'm sure."

Zeeman said to Steiner, "What's the connection between you and Sydney Popovitch?"

"Sydney-Boy and Meri…" The little man gave the chair arms a momentary rattling with his fingertips. "You could say they worked for me."

"Doin' what, Creep?"

"Smuggling."

"You hear that, Baby?"

"With interest, Tio."

"A guy with a long, pointy blade could catch Popovitch unawares, Creep. How come that didn't happen?"

"Leon got in on the action. I had to back off."

"Again with Leon," Menotti grunted.

"I'll take care of Leon, Menotti. Don't worry about him."

"You? A blind and deaf kitten could kick your ass with its crippled paw." Then the burly man faced his partner. "What say, Baby?"

"The deal is for getting the doll from Popovitch, Bad Man. If Leon cuts himself in, we get double."

The little man shrugged. "Deal."

Zeeman said, "One more thing... There's a wedding picture in the bedroom." The tall man's words came out slowly. However, there was an edge to his voice. "I'm assuming Popovitch is the man in the photo."

Steiner grinned. "The Errol Flynn look-alike standing next to the pretty brunette."

"How does the brunette fit in?"

"Deidre doesn't, other than being Sydney-Boy's wife, Mr. Zeeman." The little man adjusted this sunglasses. "You don't like the idea of roughing up a woman?"

"Baby, I'm not getting tough with a broad."

"Why Menotti. Meri said you threatened to kill her."

"That was different, Creep."

Zeeman put his hands on his hips and studied the man in the foil hat for a long moment. Then he said, "Maybe the doll's here?"

"I searched, Mr. Zeeman. No doll."

"There's searching and then there's searching, Creep." The burly man's eyebrows shot up in question. "You want me to tear this place apart, Baby?"

"We can do that after Popovitch heads for Hull."

"What if he don't take his wife?"

"Trust me, Tio. The way she looks, only a dead man would leave her home." Zeeman moved closer to the little man. "Meri and Sydney had a thing for quite some time?"

Steiner made an enclosure for his thumbs with his fingers. "When it comes to women, I don't mind sharing. Why?"

"I've got this nagging feeling that I'm missing something."

"You'd better not be playing us, Creep."

"Relax, Menotti."

"Where are the Popovitchs, Bad Man?"

"Out."

"Out where, Creep?"

"Out where they won't get under foot." The little man checked his watch. "We're runnin' past time."

"You're sure 'bout tomorrow being game day?"

"I'm sure, Menotti."

"What's to keep Popovitch from going to Hull without the doll?"

"He won't." Steiner got to his feet. "He takes the doll every place he goes."

"What makes you think you got the straight dope on Hull, Creep?"

"Radar, Menotti." The little man tightened the foil cap against his skull. "Heard everything on the radar."

"You believe him, Baby?"

The sound of a cane-tapping came from outside. The three men turned toward the kitchen windows. A beautiful brunette moved across the sidewalk with the aid of a white cane. She wore a brown suit with a high-necked white blouse, white stockings, and brown shoes and had pulled her hair in a bun.

"Who's that?" Menotti demanded.

"Deidre Popovitch," Steiner replied. "She's home early. Bitch's blind. But, as you can see, she's got a body that won't quit." He made the slurping sound. "Makes my dick beg to get outa' my pants, and past hers."

"That wedding picture doesn't do her justice," Zeeman breathed.

From the tall man's perspective, Mrs. Popovitch was near-perfection. Her sightless eyes were large and almond shaped. Her face was a perfect oval, milky-white. Her delicate features might have been formed from flawless marble. He judged her to be about thirty-five. She reminded him of the prim and proper school teacher he had when he was in first grade. The one who had kissed his cheek to make everything better after a six grader had punched him.

"I'd give my left nut for her, Tio."

"Baby, this ain't no time for impulsive commitments."

"Time to boogey, gentlemen." The little man pointed toward the stairway to the apartment door. "One of the doors in the hall leads to the upper floors. We'll pop up one flight and slip out the front door. The bitch'll never know we were here."

Chapter 3
"A Discussion"

Carmine Street was one of many dimly lit roadways in Beacon Hill. Number 32 boasted a streetlamp out front as well as red and green neon on its white face. The latter advertised *Froggy's Pizza*. A beer advert dangled in the cafe's front window showing a brunette in an overstuffed bikini. Fluorescent-light struggled to get past the sign like a blue flare. Scents, from crushed herbs and spiced meats, permeated the night air around the building.

"You gonna' tell me where you went, tonight?" Menotti asked.

"Errand," Zeeman said impatiently. "Where were you when I got back?"

"Went for a walk. No sense hangin' 'round if you're out."

The two men occupied a small table at the rear of the restaurant. Menotti was devouring a pepperoni pizza. Zeeman picked at a thick square of cheese-oozing lasagna.

"Three hours, you were gone." Menotti waggled a slice. "That's some errand."

"Where'd you get three hours?"

"I can read a watch."

"But, you didn't get back until an hour after I got home."

"I saw you get out of the taxi." The burly man filled his mouth, again. He masticated for a few moments. Then he said, "You been on a knife-edge since that errand. If I was a betting man, I'd say something went south."

"Let it go, Tio."

"Baby, there's business and then there's business." The burly man's face went dark, his brows drawn together. "Right now, you and me got business with a nut-job in a foil cap." Menotti took another bite of pizza, and then chewed out, "If the Creep figured into your errand, I got a right to know."

"I said, let it go."

"The phone rang just before you went out. Was it him?"

Zeeman tilted his head to one side, toying at the lasagna rather than eating it. Realizing that an explanation was unavoidable he eventually said, "Meri."

"That's where you went?" Menotti gaped. "To see Meri?"

"Yeah."

"You didn't think I'd wanna' go along?"

"Meri didn't want you there," the big man snapped.

"What do you mean, she didn't want me there?" A flicker of jealousy crossed the burly man's round face. "'Course she wanted me there." His right hand moved, the pizza slice cutting a path back and forth through the air. "Why wouldn't she want me there?"

"It's complicated."

"Since when can't I handle complicated?"

Exasperated, Zeeman shoved his meal off to one side. "This is exactly why I didn't want to get into it."

"What happened? Meri got on her high horse 'cause I threatened to kill her?" The burly man shook the slice at his partner. "You threatened to kill her, too."

"Tio, she didn't want you involved."

"Since when can't I get involved?" Menotti shifted in his chair, lowering his chin in a pout. "You talked business?"

"Strictly business."

"So, we're okay with her?"

"What do you mean?"

"Forgive and forget."

"Meri agrees there were mistakes. She wants to put it behind us. I agreed."

"So, you told her we'd forgive and forget?"

"Everything's settled, Tio."

Menotti maneuvered his bulk on the chair cushion for a few uncomfortable seconds. Then, his voice rose sharply. "Meri asked 'bout me, right?"

"Of course she asked."

"So she still thinks 'bout me?"

"How can she not think about you?" Zeeman returned, with a feeble grin. "You and Meri have the ass-grab thing."

Menotti dropped the pizza slice to his plate, leaned back in his chair, his chin bobbing, his lips pursed. He sat in silence for a long moment, like that, thinking. Then a brightness came to his bulldog face, and he tilted forward; leaning his forearms atop the table.

"That's what makes what her and me got special." His chin bobbed, again, emphasizing his statement. His lips spread in a smile. "We're soul mates."

"Meri told you that?" Zeeman squinted across the table at his partner.

"Not in as many words. But she did say I was a virtuoso with the pinching pinkies." Menotti picked up the partially eaten slice and took a big bite. "I chalk that up to them piano lessons I took."

"What lessons?"

"Them two lessons I took, when I was twelve."

"Ah, those lessons."

"You remember, now?"

"I remember the last lesson." Zeeman shifted in his chair, tilting back and crossing his long legs. "You sat in front of the piano in the church basement, your pinching pinkies tickling the ivories. The reverend Jones, who was teaching you, went to the kitchen to get a cup of coffee. Then, while you tinkled chopsticks, I rolled the piano out the back door and into my old man's waiting van. You were still playing as Pops drove off." A strand of humor teased the corners of his mouth. "We got forty buck for that piano."

Menotti grabbed another slice of pizza. "Uh, when's Meri coming by?"

"She's not."

"Sure she's coming by." The burly man's voice quivered with hurt and disappointment. "Why wouldn't she come by? You said you'd fixed things."

"Meri's got trouble with Bad Man."

"What trouble?"

"I said it was complicated."

"If Meri's got trouble with the Creep, I'll take care of it." The unfinished slice hit the plate. "That's what her and me and you are about. We take care of each other."

"When we're not threatening to kill her, you mean?"

"Well, that goes without saying." The burly man wiped his face and hands on a napkin. "Why ain't she coming by?"

"Like Bad Man said, there are complications."

"Nothing complicated about it. I bust the Creep's head. You put a round in his eye." The burly man's eyes narrowed on his partner. "Baby, in five seconds it's a done deal."

"That takes out Bad Man. But it doesn't solve her problem."

"How can it not solve her problem? The Creep'll be dead."

"Killing him isn't enough."

"Okay. If she wants his sorry ass tortured, I'll torture. What's Meri want done to him?"

"I said it was complicated, not weird."

"Then, how 'bout we uncomplicate it?" Menotti snapped.

Zeeman glanced around before confiding, "Bad Man tried to kill Meri."

"Is she okay?"

"So far. But, he's looking for her."

"When did this go down?"

"A couple of weeks ago."

"But, that was before we got out. Before we met with the Creep." The burly man made a disgusted face. "What did the Creep do? Go after her with whips and shit?"

"My point is, Bad Man wants Meri dead."

Menotti's face hardened, his lips tight. "The bastard sat there and played us, Baby. The doll was just a scam hoping we'd lead him to her."

"The doll's real enough. So is Popovitch having it."

"Baby, I don't follow."

"The doll belongs to Nikolay Kandinsky. If Bad Man doesn't get it to Kandinsky, the Russian will put a price on Bad Man's head."

There was a bout of strained silence.

"Russian Mafia Nikolay Kandinsky?" Menotti croaked.

"There's only one Kandinsky."

Menotti cleared his throat twice. "So, if I'm understanding all this, the Creep works for Kandinsky?"

"Not only works for the Russian, but, Bad Man's setting you and me up for a hit by the Kandinsky's goons."

"What for?"

"To dump the blame on the doll having gone missing, on us."

"But, we're going to get it back."

"Not if things go as planned for Bad Man."

"What do you mean?"

"Once we get the doll from Popovitch, Bad Man plans to fake his own death. He'll disappear with the doll and we'll be fitted into the frame for doing it. Kandinsky will come after us like the proverbial Russian bear."

"What's the matter with Popovitch as the bear's meat?"

"Don't you remember Bad Man's five grand offer for us to whack Popovitch?"

There was another stretch of silence. Then Tio Menotti slowly nodded. "We take out Popovitch, and that becomes confirmation of the Creep's death, after he disappears. Kandinsky won't turn a cog to find the Creep. He and his goons'll be too busy tearing us apart." He gulped several times. "Baby, I'm not liking what I'm saying."

"Now do you understand why I said it was complicated?"

The burly man breathed in and out to trying to quiet his nerves. But the tension remained in his face.

"Baby, I say we cut cable and catch wind."

"If it was just you and me, I'd agree. But, there's Meri to consider. We can't leave her for the Russian to pluck."

"Why not? Baby, it ain't like she didn't hang you and me out to dry?"

Zeeman's smile was bittersweet. "What happened to forgive and forget?"

"That was before the Creep put our asses in a sling with Kandinsky!" The burly man wagged his head morosely, his voice a high whimper. "I told you we shouldn't hook up with Meri. I told you this whole gig was setup."

"There's still another wrinkle to her problem."

"Sweet Jesus! You mean it gets worse?"

"Not worse. Just more complicated."

"Baby, it can't get more complicated."

"Sydney Popovitch is running his own game on Meri."

"What game?"

Zeeman dragged fingers through his dark hair. "He plans to finger Meri, to Kandinsky, for stealing the doll unless Meri kills Popovitch's wife."

"Kill that beautiful Blind Lady?"

"As far as I know, that's the only wife Popovitch has."

"So, if we don't take out Popovitch then Meri'll be on the Russian's hit list." Menotti's hands became fists on the tabletop. "Only if we take him out, we'll become Russian teacakes."

"Happy that you got me to spill?"

"If the Russian's the stick, what's the carrot for Meri making the hit on the Blind Lady?"

"Popovitch hands the doll to Meri."

"She gives it to Kandinsky. That gets her off the hook with the Russian, which means the Kandinsky would give her protection from Bad Man. Only Bad Man will be sitting in the wings, waiting to make a move on her as soon as she gets the doll."

"Unless we get the doll first, and take out Bad Man before Kandinsky gets back to town."

"He's out of town?"

"The Russian's in Florida. Supposed to be back in the next week, or two."

Menotti chewed his lip, thinking. "Popovitch has a life insurance on the Blind Lady?"

"Two million. Double indemnity if she's murdered."

"That's a lot of money."

"She's a lot of woman."

"Money aside, why's he want to get clear of a pretty woman like her?"

"The same 'why' that's been dogging marriages since the beginning of time: Another woman."

"That Blind Lady went lesbo?"

"Popovitch has the roving eye."

"He oughta' take a closer look at what he's already got."

"Unfortunately, his heart and wedding tackle are set on someone else."

"I take it the new broad ain't interested in a guy with empty pockets?"

"Not much."

There was another span of silence. Then, the burly man drew in his breath sharply. "Who's the new fox?"

"Remember that girl we saw coming out of the building when we arrived at 5-B Derne?"

"That kid?" Menotti's eyebrows shot up his face showing disgust and disbelief. "She can't be no more than twelve."

"Meri says she's legal."

"Baby, there's legal and then there's legal and what I saw ain't legal even if she is legal."

"That's part of your charm, Tio. Every now and then you get a twinge of morality."

"What do you mean, twinge? I went to church."

"Yeah. For them two lessons so you and me and my old man could steal that piano."

"It still counts."

Silence fell between the men.

"Baby, this ain't kosher."

"You wanted Italian."

"I'm talking about that doll." Menotti hesitated. "The Creep said he was in the smuggling racket, right?"

"That's what he said, Tio."

"And we believed him, right?"

"It was a stretch."

"Well, assuming the Creep didn't stretch the truth too far, that doll's gotta' be stuffed with something."

"My words to Meri."

"And?"

"Bling-blings."

The burly man's eyes got big and round. "Faceted diamonds?"

"Meri values the bundle at a million."

"A real million, Baby?" Menotti gave his partner an avaricious look. "Not monopoly money?"

"Long green, Tio."

The burly man's brow puckered. "We could short circuit this whole gig and come out with pockets stuffed."

"Your plan being?"

"We take out Popovitch, the Creep and Kandinsky." He wetted his lips, greedily. "Then you, me and Meri and that damn doll head for California."

"I like the sound of it, Tio."

A momentary smile came to the burly man's face. "As a bonus, nobody'd touch that beautiful Blind Lady."

"Another nice tone."

"Baby, you and me deserve two-thirds of a million."

"No argument, Tio. But we'll have to settle for half a mill."

"Half?" The burly man blinked several times. "Why half?"

"I already cut a deal with Meri. Her end is half the Bling-blings."

"Where does she come off wanting half?" the burly man sputtered. "We've always done a three-way split."

"Not this time."

"Baby, you and me are clearing the decks. What's Meri bringing to the table, other than her complications with the Creep?"

"It's a done deal, Tio."

The burly man pouted for a few seconds. Then he said, "Okay, she gets half. No big deal." His heavy shoulders heaved. "Half's fine. No problem. I can dig it. Meri comes out on top and we get screwed." He nibbled his lip a moment. "How does it play out?"

"We know from Bad Man that Popovitch is sending his wife to Hull this Friday. Meri will get there a day ahead as part of Popovitch's plan to kill Blind Lady. Popovitch won't head for Hull until Saturday. That leaves him at home, alone. You and I show up at Popovitch's flat as follow-through with Bad Man's plans. We do our number on Popovitch and get the doll. Then, before we head for Hull we take care of Bad Man. After that you take the doll and hook up with Meri. I know a guy in San Francisco who will take the Bling-blings off our hands for ten percent, provided they're not laser-numbered. You take our end and head there."

"And if they are lasered?"

"You'll have to negotiate the best deal you can."

"What about you?"

"I'll stay behind to deal with Kandinsky when he gets back into town."

The burly man went stiff with the effort to control his concerns. "Baby, you can't take on Kandinsky alone."

"I've got something special planned for the Russian."

"Baby, Nikolay Kandinsky never goes anywhere alone. His goons carry automatic weapons. Your snub-nose .38 won't even make those guys blink."

"ANFO."

An elderly man entered the café, a brass-topped cane bearing the weight on the fellow's right side. He hobbled over to a table not far from where Menotti and Zeeman sat.

"Explosives are good." The burly man nodded his bald head agreeably. "I'll rig a cell-phone controller. We can place it under his car before we connect with the Creep. No need for you to hang around after we get the doll. We both got to San Francisco and you make a long distance call. Boom."

Zeeman smiled very slightly. "No guaranty the Russian will be in the car when I make that call. The only sure tactic is to wait, watch and make that call when he gets in."

"I see your point, Baby. But, I still don't like you being here alone."

"How long will it take you to get what we need for the bomb?"

"Fertilizer and diesel fuel are no problem. A couple of throw-away phones are easy enough. The detonator's the only issue." Menotti scratched the stubble on his chin. "I could build one using picric acid. All I'll need is an empty cartridge case, fuse, Aspirin, sulfuric acid and sodium nitrate."

"Or, we could use a hobby-shop rocket detonator."

"Then it's down to when. Did Meri give you a date for the Russian's homecoming?"

"Could be tomorrow. Could be a week from tomorrow. She didn't know."

"I guess you'll just have to hang loose." The burly man wiped his mouth with a napkin. "Baby, tell me something... What's wrong with me?"

"I've got no complaints."

"I'm talkin' 'bout me and women."

Zeeman chuckled softly. "Tio, you just have to find the right one."

"I know that. What bothers me is why Meri hooked up with the Creep?"

"She didn't have a choice."

"Baby, everybody's got a choice. And when it comes to choices, the Creep shouldn't be in the running."

"Meri was in a bind after we were sent up. She'd run a tab with Kandinsky."

"She was chasing the nags, again?"

"When wasn't she?" Zeeman tilted forward, leaning his forearms on the tabletop. "And, as per usual, Meri was not one for picking the winner. When she couldn't come up with the money, to cover her losses, the Russian gave her the option of working off the debt or a swim in the Atlantic wearing cement water-wings."

"Meri's never been much for swimming."

"Exactly. Which is when the Russian introduced her to Bad Man."

"But, Kandinsky wouldn't have told her to screw the Creep."

Zeeman eased back in his chair, nodding. "That point I'll give you."

"How'd she latch onto Popovitch?"

"Popovitch was already working for Bad Man," Zeeman explained. "They were bringing stuff from Indonesia to Paris, and then from Paris to Boston: watches, artifacts, gems—whatever the Russian wanted." Zeeman smiled without pleasure. "That's how Popovitch was able to con her over the doll."

"The Creep always uses a doll for smuggling?"

"It's strictly for gemstones."

"How is it Customs didn't x-ray it?"

"I'm sure they did. But, the doll has a thick, steel-tube frame. The stones are dumped into the tubing, then the tubing is filled with hot wax." The shadow of a smile tickled the tall man's lips. "The wax keeps the diamonds from rattling during transit. And all an x-ray catches is what looks like a solid steel frame."

The burly man pulled a cigar from his suit, and lit it. "How'd Meri look?"

"Scared."

"The Creep's hat would scare anybody." Menotti's hands rose and fell with exasperation. "Damn it Baby, Meri's screwing everybody but me."

"Stop sounding rejected, Tio."

"I *am* rejected."

The tall man offered his partner a crooked smile. "Meri looked better than she was."

"Maybe she wasn't a sexual rock star, as far as you're concerned, but I'd settle for her." The burly man took a sip of wine. As he returned the glass to the table, his mind did another turn. "Why make all this complication?"

"That went past me, Tio."

"Why send Blind Lady to Hull?" Menotti splayed his hands. "Why not kill her, here?"

"According to Meri the Sheriff in Hull is a brain-dead bozo. His name's Dave Sherman. He's never investigated a homicide and he's the type who doesn't ask for help."

"Meaning Blind Lady's killing wouldn't be solved."

"All but guaranteed."

The burly man glanced around the café. The man with the cane was giving a waitress his order. Other patrons were either sipping beer or wine or chit-chatting. After another scan of the room, Menotti refocused on Zeeman.

"Baby, I still don't understand Popovitch's reasoning?"

"What's to understand? He wants a younger woman."

"I mean, why risk having his wife killed? Popovitch already has a million in diamonds. Why not do a runner with that?"

"Double indemnity will get him four times that."

"Only if he doesn't get nailed for the killing."

"Taking the diamonds will put Kandinsky on his trail. I don't think Popovitch has the stones to take on the Russian."

The burly man meshed his fingers as he eased back in the chair, his hands hitting his belly, his face grim. "What made Meri and Popovitch wait until now to run their game?"

"Tourists."

"Come again?"

"According to Meri, this is the first week, all year, that Popovitch's Bed and Breakfast, in Hull, hasn't been overrun with guests. No guests. No witnesses to the Blind Lady's murder."

"Popovitch owns a resort?"

"His father does."

"Does the old man know what's planned?"

"I doubt it. When do parents ever know the dirt their kids get up to?"

"My mom did. Your old man did, too."

"But, we came from different stock."

Menotti nodded, agreeably. "Did I tell you my mom's getting out next June?"

"I thought she was serving life without parole?"

"The outgoing governor commuted her sentence."

"How'd she arrange that?"

"A friend of hers caught the governor on video doing something he oughtn't do, if he wants to stay clear of jail."

"I always said your mom was a woman of rare vintage."
"Pop said the same thing, God rest his soul."

Chapter 4
"News of a Murder"

"*Dobriy vecher*, Deidre Popovitch."

Serge Vasiliev, a square-set Russian, was descending the steps from the main entrance of 5 Derne Street toward the front sidewalk. Vasiliev wore a dated, but neatly-pressed, gray suit and shiny black shoes. His shirt was a darker shade of gray. His beard-line looked grayish in the morning sunshine. He had thick, wide lips, also grayish in hue. Over one arm he'd draped a bulky, gray overcoat. Pink socks and a pink Windsor punctuated his gray figure. Vasiliev's self-confident movements and neat attire suggested a man of breeding and intellect.

"What brings you into this depressing chill, Serge?" Deidre called back.

She was standing at the top of the steps from the basement facing the sidewalk, trying to catch her breath. A blue, knitted dress clung to her firm figure. White shoes encased her feet. The cold air gave her cheeks a pink hue. Her breath came out in white clouds. Under her left arm she carried two garbage bags. Her right hand gripped her white cane.

"I someone meet," the elderly man said.

When the Russian reached the sidewalk, he stopped and slipped on his overcoat. As he buttoned it, an expectant Vasiliev looked up and down the avenue.

"Lucky you." Deidre moved forward, blindly juggling the bags. "I'm freezing my patootie dumping trash."

"Why not Sydney do? He broke arms got?"

"Sydney's packing." Her narrow shoulders quivered because of the chilly air. "We're going to Hull."

"Armpit of Massachusetts."

"It wasn't my choice."

"Vacation?"

"Second honeymoon."

The elderly Russian frowned in confusion. "*Second honeymoon?*"

"It's what married couples do before they divorce."

"Ah, understanding." A ghost of a smile twisted his mouth. "Chance last to kill loved-one."

"I'm told murder's a common outcome." The blind woman continue across the wide footway. "In my case inevitable."

"What say?"

"My husband is planning to kill me."

His head wagged in disbelief. "No so."

"It came as a surprise to me, too." Deidre took a deep breath and let it out a plume of white, as she tapped onward. "I knew our marriage wasn't perfect. But, I thought it was working–more or less."

"Stop," the old man cried as she tapped past the trash cans.

In five, surprisingly quick strides Serge Vasiliev stood next to her. Then, one of his huge hands gripped her arm to stop the blind woman from stumbling off the curb, into the street. Her mouth dropped open in surprise at his abrupt handling.

"What's wrong?" she demanded.

"Get too far, Deidre Popovitch. Near road. Get car-smacked big time."

"*Bla-go-dar-iu.*"

"Welcome." Vasiliev snatched the bags from her with his free hand, and escorted the blind woman back to the trash bins. "Good Russian you got."

"Thanks to your excellent tutelage." She smiled at nothing in particular. "I've become particularly proficient with the naughty words."

"Best ones."

The Russian deposited her bundles in a trash bin. Then he accompanied the blind woman back to the steps leading down to her flat.

"You shouldn't be so gallant, Serge," Deidre declared. "I might seduce you."

"Mit me, okay," he returned, with a grin. "But, Sydney not like."

She curled her arms about her waist, trying to conserve body heat. "Sydney went off me after we exchanged vows. *Ya nye zna-yu, chto so mnoi.*"

"Him little blue pill needing."

"Money's become Sydney's only interest." She hefted her shoulders in an exaggerated shrug. "The insurance policy on my life will be his shortcut to a fortune if my husband has his way." A gust of icy wind gave Deidre another shiver. "But he won't. I'm going to crush his murder-plan."

"Murder-plan not need crush. Better Sydney's balls in vice." He held up one hand, palm toward her, extending all five digits. "Moscow, I four times marry to avoid vice."

"You told me six." Her eyes darted blindly toward his voice. "Were you bragging about your sexual conquests?"

"Four times. Six times." Vasiliev shrugged. "After two, what difference is?"

"One marriage has provided enough misery for my lifetime." A chilly smile hovered over Deidre's tight lips. "I hear your body twisting back and forth. Who are you looking for?"

"Meet young chick."

The blind woman smiled. "Romance is flitting on the wing?"

"She come. We go. Big time."

"You said, 'young chick.' How old is your passion flower?"

"Sixty-two. Big *sai-zi*."

"I'm glad she's well endowed."

"So is Vasiliev." The elderly man's eyes squinted as he checked the street, again. "If Sydney gone off, who to gone?"

"If I told you, you'd never believe me."

"Vasiliev from Siberia. Believe anything."

There was another gust of cold wind. In response, Deidre clutched her forearms across her breasts.

"Sydney's having an affair with a woman who has a doll fetish." The blind woman grimaced in self-pity. "I hate dolls. They remind me of dead babies."

"Blow up dolls no fun for Serge." The Russian made a snort of disgust. "*Khryen* not like cold rubber."

"It's my fervent belief is that most men's privates prefer the real deal. But in this case, the doll is not a toy for kinky fun. It's a toy created for a child."

"Ah, better sense make." He frowned at her. "What make other woman special?"

"I haven't met her, yet." She dropped the tenor of her voice, reflecting deep anger. "But, I'm going to do my best to kill her."

The old man studied the blind woman, his eyes showing pity and concern. "Deidre not kill. Too good person."

"Nonsense. Just because I'm blind shouldn't preclude me from having a good time at the expense of others." Her chin dipped and rose with determination. "That's the American way."

"Take from Vasiliev, kill no fun."

"That depends on who's dying at the time."

He made a worried face at her. "Joke, big time?"

"Remember a couple of weeks ago when you set up that recorder and cell-phone for me? Then you sneaked that call-monitoring software onto Sydney's cell-phone?"

"You ask. I help."

"Sydney's new love is going to kill me after I get to Hull. I heard them discussing it." She licked her lips, twice. "That woman sounds quite clever for the average doll-loving slut."

"Go police."

"I want them dead."

"They suffer time long in jail. Go police."

She smiled at no one. "I hadn't considered that."

"In jail, Sydney become boy-toy to man named Lavonia or Justine or Beatrice."

"That would be delicious."

"Damn sweeter than kill Sydney."

"I'm still in the planning stage, so don't blow a gasket."

He looked down at his feet. "Take boat or train to Hull?"

"The afternoon ferry."

"Train more private for killer. Toss off boat got good possibles. You sure they wait for Hull?"

"I'm sure."

He raised his head and waggled a finger. "You not back, fix Sydney, big time. I got vice in workroom size of T32 tank. Squeeze balls to jelly."

"Keep the thought. But, I'll be back." The blind woman started down the steps and then turned back. "Any news about that murdered woman?"

"Hear plenty." He fingered his chin for a moment. "Radio sob-story, big time. Ever-body worry. Crazed woman killer looser. Parking lots no safe."

"According to everyone at the grocers it's a clear case of little green space travelers having a predisposition for sexual kinks. Edgar Hampton, in the meat department, claims to have irrefutable proof."

"Like old cable, Hampton one with kinks."

"I've heard that, too." The blind woman spoke rapidly not pausing for breath. "According to Mrs. Hampton, her husband's exceedingly well-informed on female sexual dominance, which requires his wife to wear a red corset leather boots and crack a whip on his bare backside, not that I'd object to doing so in Sydney's case if there was a chance in hell he would suffer eternal testicular inflammation." The blind woman licked her lips from corner to corner. Then the tempo of Deidre's voice fell into a soft tenor filled with curiosity. "In your vast experience, Serge, as a Siberian Casanova, have you ever come across a sexually dominant woman?"

"Second wife. She from Smolensk." There was a lilt in the Russian's voice, as if fond memories had overtaken him. "Smolensk woman get first whip, when just girl. Tradition, big time."

"Sounds like practical early planning to cure innate flaws in the male sex."

"Second wife teethed on hers." Then he rubbernecked toward the sound of an approaching car. "Whip you got?"

She shook her dark head. "But Mrs. Hampton told me about something called a Cat of Nine Tails. It sounded like the solution to all of Sydney's problems."

"Second wife have." He nodded agreeably. "Nine lead balls tipping leather flails. Very painful."

"Sounds excruciatingly perfect." The blind woman paused a beat, frowning in thought. "Do whips come in colors?"

"Crack ass. Get color, big time."

"We must record your exploits some day. I think the world would find them fascinating." She shuddered in the cold. "Have the police identified the dead woman?"

"Meri Darling."

The blind woman's mouth dropped open. For many silent seconds she gaped. "Serge, are you sure about the name?"

"Sure as police sure." Vasiliev drew in a breath, then let it out with a vaporous sigh. "Not live 'round here."

"Meri Darling was Sydney's lover."

He gave the blind woman a startled look. "Doll lady? Sure?"

"There can't be many women named Meri Darling."

"Maybe Sydney kill?"

She raised her hands to her mouth, cupping them across her lips and blowing warmth on her fingers. "Why would Sydney kill Meri when Sydney wants her to kill me?"

"Sydney not strange to foot shoot."

"That's an understatement." She wet her lips. "You could be right. Sydney was out last night. When he got home, he wouldn't tell me where he'd been." Deidre fanned the air with both hands. "I'm being ridiculous."

"Not so ridiculous."

"What's your new love's name, Serge?"

"Dasha."

"That doesn't sound Bostonian."

"Smolensk."

The blind woman chuckled. "Will Dasha bring her whip collection on your outing?"

"Big time." He laughed.

She resumed her movements down the steps. Over one shoulder she called, "Tell Dasha from me: *Ne pro-pa-dai!*"

"I tell."

Chapter 5
"Admission"

When Deidre Popovitch reached her apartment, she tried the doorknob. It would not turn. Irritated, the blind woman gave the wood a sharp triple-rap with her cane.

"Sydney!" she cried out.

From inside the apartment her husband's voice responded with a hesitant, "Deidre?"

"Who else, Sydney? Who else would bang on the door, call your name, and demand to come in order to save her freezing nipples?"

"Yeah. Coming."

Unhurried footpads shuffled up the steps to the door. Sydney Popovitch pulled it open, and stepped back. He had a cellular phone in one hand.

"Sorry," Popovitch muttered.

He was six feet tall, well-tanned, solidly built, wide in the shoulders and narrow of hip. He was just past forty and gray mingled in his closely-trimmed blond hair. In khaki cloth and western boots, he looked like a big-game hunter out of a fifty's film.

"Why was the damn door locked?" Deidre complained.

"It creaked open after you left." Her husband shoved the phone into a pocket. "It must've locked when I pushed it shut."

"One more thing, in our marriage, that doesn't work."

The blind woman stepped forward with one hand outstretched searching for the stair-railing, the other holding her cane. Her husband backed out of the way without providing assistance.

"Are we packed?" Deidre let her impatience show.

"Almost." Popovitch shut the door, passed his wife, and quickly descended the steps to the front room. "Couple more things for the big suitcase."

"As long as you're carrying it, put in what you like."

Deidre followed the railing down, her step-treading slow but steady, her cane bouncing on each stair.

"At the ferry I'll get you a porter," her husband remarked.

"Porters don't work for free, Sydney," she snapped. "What's wrong with your back?"

"I won't be going with you to Hull."

There was dead silence as the blind woman's mouth silently worked in stupefied shock. Finally Deidre blurted, "Why in hell not?"

"I took a job."

"A job?" She was at the stair-bottom facing her husband's voice. "We're supposed to be going on a second honeymoon."

"Deidre, I couldn't turn it down."

"You arrange a weekend in what Serge calls the armpit of Massachusetts, and then you send me alone?"

"I'll be there. It's just that I'll be delayed a day: maybe two."

"My dream come true, Sydney. A honeymoon by myself."

Popovitch stared at his feet, struggling to control his temper.

"Deidre, we agreed to make an earnest effort at reconciliation." s His eyes went back to her as he lit a cigarette. "Your snide comments aren't helping."

"You and I agreed to a lot of things, Sydney. Most of which you either forgot or ignored. So, don't give me grief over a little sarcasm."

The blind woman tapped her way toward the kitchen.

"What's your panic?" Popovitch demanded. "I'll get you seated on the ferry. Pop will meet you when it docks." He made a pleading gesture with both hands. "He'll drive you to the bed and breakfast. He'll take you to our cabin."

"Wonderful." Deidre's voice dripped with emotion. "I can't wait to leave."

"What's the big deal?"

The blind woman banged into the stove and stopped.

"The big deal, Sydney, is that I get to spend twenty minutes alone on the deck of a leaking tub. Then I get to sit alone in a seaside shit-hole." A flush of frustration colored her face. Deidre's lips turned down as if she might cry. "Can we do this every year?"

"You're the one who's always saying how we need our own space."

"Let me make a note of your heartfelt concerns in my happiness-diary."

"We're short on money. What am I supposed to do?"

She fumbled along the top of the stove searching for the teakettle.

"Are you expecting cash from this business venture, Sydney? Or will it fall apart, as usual, leaving me and my unemployment checks to carry the proverbial can?"

Popovitch's lips tightened, livid colors streaked his cheeks. "This deal will turn a bundle."

"Sydney, if I had a nickel for every time you've said that, we'd have bundles up the ying-yang." Finding the object of her search the blind woman picked up the aluminum container, tapped over to the sink and dumped out the water. "What's the company's name?"

Her husband hesitated, as if having trouble recalling details. "Uh, Allied Services."

"Why is it, Sydney, that every time you get a contract it's with a company I've never heard of?"

"Allied Services is a big distribution company."

The blind woman turned on the tap, and let the water flow into the kettle.

"Distributors of what?" she called, over one shoulder.

"Freight contractor."

"What do they freight?"

"Deidre, they haul all kinds of stuff."

"Okay, Sydney." She smiled twistedly, turning off the water. "If this freight company is such a jewel, why do they need you?"

Popovitch drew in his breath and let it out in a long, frustrated sigh. "Allied Services wants a new data entry and retrieval system."

"But, why you? Why not somebody from their programming staff?" She turned toward his voice, still holding the teakettle. "Surely such a successful concern has a programming staff?"

"Allied requested a complicated system. I have a great deal more experience than their staff."

"But, why you of all the people in the world?"

"Why are you interrogating me?"

"I'm trying to understand why this great company didn't contact one of the big consulting firms?"

He thumped his chest with a finger. "I don't have to justify anything."

"Of course you do, Sydney. I'm your wife. The woman you vowed to love and honor. The woman who wonders what her husband gets up to when he's out at all hours?"

"I'm not getting up to anything!"

"Of course you are, Sydney. You're always up to something."

Deidre tapped her way back to the stove, and set the teakettle on top of a burner.

"Since when?" he demanded.

"Let's start with a recent situation. That woman who keeps calling. What's her name? Meri Darling?"

The blind woman switched on the burner's heating element.

"You're blaming me because somebody calls?" he demanded.

"She called for you. Who else could be to blame?"

Popovitch looked around, rising anger evident in his body language. "To be fair, Deidre…"

She cut in, bitterly with, "Surely, we're not going to have our traditional 'fairness' discussion?"

"Fine. Fine. I'm at fault. As usual, put the blame on my sorry ass."

"Thank you, Sydney. That is where our marital problems belong."

Deidre stood erect reaching her hand over the stove until she found the teakettle. Her fingers slid over the heating vessel until she located the spout. Not feeling any steam, Deidre leaned back against the counter.

"Look, I'm sorry about the job's timing." Sydney's chin dipped and he looked at her, again. "It's just that…"

"That's another thing, Sydney," she intervened. "Your bad timing. I'm amazed at its consistency. No matter how I'm involved, your timing screws up my good time."

"Fine. Fine. I'm a screw up. Why don't you just nail me to a cross?"

"If only that could be, Sydney." Then the blind woman faced her husband's voice. "I know about your affair."

"Wh—what affair?"

"Do you think I'm stupid, Sydney?"

"Damn it, Deidre, I have no idea what you're talking about."

"Presumed innocence?" The blind woman let go a sour laugh. "Would you like me to read you your rights, Sydney?" An amused expression flickered across Deidre's face. "I may be blind, Sydney, but I know what's going on."

"Paranoid. That crazy Russian's made you paranoia!"

"Because I object to infidelity?"

"The only thing I'm doing is trying to make us a life." Popovitch began moving around the front room, his boot heels leaving black marks on the floor's linoleum. "Instead of complaining, you should be giving me credit for trying."

"All right, Sydney. I admit it. You do the best you can. Unfortunately, you suck at it. I mean, you suck at everything."

"Fine. Fine. I get the message. I suck as a provider."

"No, Sydney, you suck at everything. *Everything.*" A forced smile thinned her lips. "Well, maybe the economy will take an upward tilt, blind schools will feel a surge of federal funding, and I can go back to teaching." She purposely made an auditory sigh. "It'll be delicious to eat regularly."

Popovitch threw his hands to his hips, anger and aggravation carving his handsome face into hard lines. "Why were you so long with the garbage?"

"Now, who's interrogating?"

"I've answered all of your questions. Why not answer one of mine?"

"If you must know, I chatted with Mr. Vasiliev."

"What for?"

"Unlike you, Sydney, Serge enjoys talking with me."

"What's he been telling you?"

"Several things, including his new girlfriend," she explained. "Her name's Dasha. She's from Smolensk."

"She's probably some dog in need of a collar."

"Apparently women from that region are born with a whip fetish." The blind woman moved to the counter adjacent to the stove, leaned back against it, staring blindly ahead. "If I thought our marriage would survive, I'd ask Dasha to give you obedience training. You know the thing. Forty lashes with a cat of nine tails."

"Cat of nine tails?" His head tilted back, his eyes clenched shut. "Are you serious?"

"I told Serge about our upcoming trip or, rather, my trip. He said to tell you that if I didn't make it back, you were a dead man."

Popovitch went chalk-white as his eyes dropped to hers. "What's that supposed to mean?"

"Personally, Sydney, I'd take it as a death-threat."

"That old man's crazy. I told you he was crazy."

"Nonsense." A slightly entertained look crept over Deidre's beautiful face. "Serge's just a little weird around the edges."

"The man's culinary specialty is prune teacakes. That's more lunatic than weird."

"I think his teacakes are—well—unique." The blind woman hesitated, her face showing a flush of renewed anger. "Your rasping breath tells me that you're worried, Sydney."

"Of—of course I'm worried," Popovitch stammered. His eyes were wide with fear. "Vasiliev used to be KGB. Did you know that?"

"Nonsense." The blind woman shrugged stiffly, causing her cane to scrape along the floor. "Serge's a retired ballet instructor with pacifist leanings, and a penchant for younger women."

"And you believe that?"

"About him being a ballet instructor, yes. The rest I gleaned from Serge's wandering hands during my Russian lessons."

"That filthy old bastard's been groping you?"

"Not with any definite plan." Deidre hesitated. "Did Mr. Hampton tell you the KGB story?"

"It's no story. Serge Vasiliev was a Department 13 assassin from Moscow Central." Popovitch thrust a scolding finger at his wife. "Edgar Hampton has the straight facts on your teacake lothario."

"Mr. Hampton and Mr. Vasiliev are at war, Sydney. They've been going at it since Serge moved to the neighborhood. Just days ago, they got into a punch-up over the best brand of condoms." She grimaced, thinking. "I hope I'll have privacy during my stay at your father's bed and breakfast."

The blind woman felt her way along the kitchen counter until she located a series of tins. Deidre picked up the smallest one, turned and tapped over to the kitchen table. There she set it down.

"You'll be the only guest," he returned. "How much privacy do you need?"

"You think my desire for privacy is a joke?"

"No, I don't think it's a joke."

"Just because I'm blind, Sydney, doesn't mean I enjoy undressing in front of an open door."

"That's what this madness is about? You're angry over last year?"

"An open door that got me a round of applause from the other guests."

"You act like I did it on purpose."

The blind woman returned to the counter, reached up to the cabinets and slid her hands along until she located the one she sought. Then Deidre pulled open the door, took out a saucer and set it on the counter. Then she took out a cup, set it on the saucer, shut the door, and carried the saucer with its drinking vessel over to the table. The teakettle began to whistle. She retrieved it from the stove, and took it to the table.

"Of course you didn't do it on purpose," she said. "You accidentally went out of the room and accidently left the door wide open. This, in turn, accidentally drew the bed and breakfast's entire top floor to assess my tan while I stripped off for a bath."

"Fine. Fine," Popovitch muttered. He stalked over to the kitchen sink, dropped the cigarette butt into it, ran the tap to douse the coal, and then shut off the water. "Blame me for embarrassing you."

The blind woman sat down at the table. Deidre opened the tin and took out a teabag. She dropped it into the cup. Then, she fumbled around the table until she located the teakettle which she picked it up, pouring hot water into the cup.

"Are you having an affair with Meri Darling, Sydney?"

Popovitch gulped in shock. Then he managed to sputter, "Of course not."

"She called here, several times. Each time, I answered, she identified herself. Then, she asked to speak with you. At which time you talked to her."

"Did you tell Vasiliev about Meri Darling's calls?"

"It may have come up in conversation."

"Where did that lunatic get the idea that I was having an affair?"

"The evidence speaks for itself, Sydney."

He crept closer, squinting with concern. "What evidence?"

"Are you and Meri and planning to kill me?"

"Vasiliev told you that?"

She hesitated, purposely drawing out the silence for many seconds. Then Deidre asked, "How much am I worth to you dead?"

"Where—what—how in hell…"

"Calm down, Sydney. You sound like your heart is in your throat."

"What, exactly, did Vasiliev tell you?"

"How much life insurance do you carry on me?"

"Nothing." Her husband swallowed thickly. "We can't afford life insurance."

The blind woman offered a mocking grin. "Then I wonder what the insurance agent meant when he telephoned about a term-life policy."

"Wha—wait. I don't care what anybody said, there's no policy."

"There must be, Sydney. The man said my policy was worth two million, not counting the double indemnity clause in the event of murder. He's going to send me a copy. Before we leave, today, I'm going to call an attorney to arrange for an examination of the policy."

Popovitch mutely chewed the air, completely stunned by his wife's words, desperately wanting to speak but unable to.

"Cat got your tongue, Sydney? I can hear your mouth working. But no sound's coming out: quite unusual for you."

In a breaking cry he blurted, "Mistake!"

"What mistake, Sydney?"

"That insurance guy. He called by mistake. Mistakes happen all the time, Deidre. There's no need for an attorney."

Deidre tapped into the front room and over to the chair where her large black purse rested. She picked up the handbag and, after hooking the cane around her neck, rummaged through it.

"I don't see how it could be a mistake," she returned. "The man knew my name. Said it was on the policy. He even knew your name because you were listed as the beneficiary."

"I'm trying to save our marriage," her husband quaked, "and you're blabbering nonsense about insurance agents who don't know what they're talking about? Did you tell Vasiliev about the insurance agent?"

"Of course I did. Poor Serge got quite worked up."

"What if something happens to you? Did you consider that? What if Vasiliev calls the police? What if I'm arrested? I could end up on death row!"

"Stop with the titillating possibilities, Sydney."

"Damn it, Deidre!" After several seconds of frustrated silence, Popovitch tossed up his arms in defeat. "Fine. Fine. There is a policy. I guess I forgot to tell you. So, don't call a lawyer."

"Lucky me. I get to save those legal fees." Her hand holding the cane moved slightly. "My life is insured for two million and my husband has a faulty memory. Why insure my life, Sydney? You're the alleged bread-winner. Wouldn't it make more sense for you to carry the policy? That is how most married couples arrange their insurance needs."

He lit another cigarette, his hands trembling, his head shaking, his face showing desperation. Eventually, Popovitch said, "There was only enough money for one policy. I thought it was more important to insure your life."

"Why?"

"Why?"

"It's a simple question, Sydney. Even you should be able to answer it."

He clawed the back of his neck. "I didn't want you to worry about me, should the worst happen."

"That's so like you, Sydney. Always thinking of my feelings."

Popovitch took another draw on the cigarette and blew out a smoky series of curses. "I want you to forget about Meri Darling. I want you to forget insurance policies and any ridiculous ideas that Russian put in your head. Is that clear?"

"What about your lies? Are they a secret, too?"

After a moment of taut silence he sputtered, "When have I lied to you?"

"You always lie, Sydney. It's your stock in trade."

"Vasiliev, again?"

"What do you know about the killing down the block?" Mrs. Popovitch purposely waited for her husband to respond. When he didn't speak she continued with, "Knocked your socks off and left you dumb, did it?"

"I don't know about any murder."

"Blonde woman, not natural. Plastic tits. Nice figure. Stone dead. Left naked in a parking lot."

"Blonde... Plastic..." he muttered, in confusion. "Did Vasiliev say I killed her?"

"Serge says I'm quite eloquent in his native tongue." The blind woman took a cellular phone from her handbag. "He thinks I could hold my own with any Muscovite in the verbal abuse of my fellow beings."

"After years with you, I'm not surprised."

The blind woman returned the purse to the floor, and then punched a button on the phone. "You know, Sydney, that's as close as you've come to giving me a compliment."

A bell chimed from the phone.

"Who are you calling?" her husband demanded, his voice showing alarm.

"No one."

"Then, what're you doing?"

"Checking my phone's battery."

"What for?"

"There's no sense bringing a phone on a trip if it has a dead batter."

"There's no need to take it at all." Popovitch eyed his wife with impatience. "I'll have my phone along."

"Not for one or two days, remember? We can't have me stranded in Hull without a phone, now can we?" She laughed, tauntingly. "Besides, two phones are better than one in an emergency."

"When have we ever had an emergency?"

"Hull is infamous for power failures, Sydney. And we both know what can happen when two strangers meet in the dark." Mrs. Popovitch bent down, located her purse, returned the phone to it, and then stood erect. "Aren't you the least bit curious about the murdered woman?"

Popovitch scratched his jaw, his eyes askance.

"What's going on, Deidre? What're you up to?" He took a step toward her. "For the love of God, did Vasiliev tell the police that I killed that woman?"

"Neighborhood gossip identified the killer as a sexual anarchist from outer space. Either that or a low-level politician with moderately perverted affiliations. Personally, I'm leaning toward someone from the neighborhood. Someone the woman knew. Someone with whom she was romantically involved."

There was another bout of silence as Popovitch weighed the suggestions in his wife's statement. Then he noisily cleared his throat.

"Just—just what are you not telling me, Deidre?"

"You knew the poor woman, Sydney. *Intimately*, I think is the correct term. Although *biblically* applies."

"Did Vasiliev say that?"

"Poor, Sydney. You do have the worst luck."

"On that, I don't need reminding."

"You thought Meri Darling was the love of your life. Then she gets herself murdered."

"Murdered?" he gaped. "Meri?"

"You'll have to rework your plans for Hull, Sydney."

Popovitch staggered into the front room and sagged onto the davenport; his face without color; his breathing ragged; his Adams apple bobbing.

"You've gone pale, Sydney. Blind people aren't supposed to be able to assess coloration. But, the sounds of your constricting capillaries tell me that you've gone dead white."

He sat in silence, thinking, for several minutes. Then Popovitch asked, "What time was Meri killed?"

"I don't know."

"Who found the body?"

"Mr. Hampton's second cousin." She gave a decisive nod. A beat later Deidre shook her head. "No, I lie. It was his nephew, Fernando, the Peeping Tom."

A furrow formed across his brow, as he twisted toward his wife. "Hampton's related to a Peeping Tom?"

"Give the family credit, Sydney. The peeper's hobby is the reason Meri's body was spotted so quickly." Deidre arched her dark brows, forming bars in her forehead. "Was it the doll? That doll Meri kept calling about? Is that why you killed her, Sydney?"

Popovitch jumped up, thrusting a finger at his wife. "As far as you're concerned, there were no calls and that doll never existed."

He started pacing in front of the davenport.

"Sydney, you didn't rape the poor woman before killing her, did you?" The blind woman gave her dark head a fervent shake. "I couldn't possibly remain married to a rapist." She made a disgusted face. "Swear, to God, that you didn't rape her corpse. Sydney, I couldn't stand knowing that you prefer dead bodies to mine."

"I had it worked out." Popovitch's movements faltered and then stopped; gray streaks of trauma remapping his face. "I told her to sit tight. All we needed was one more lousy weekend." He restarted his movements, his arms rising and falling. "Fine. Fine. I'll do it myself. It won't be clean. But it'll work. The money'll be the same. That's the important thing."

The blind woman turned and tapped into the kitchen. Upon reaching the table, she sat down in front of her cup of tea and removed the teabag. Then she set it on the saucer, her beautiful face taking on an expression of self-satisfaction as she lifted the cup to her lips.

"The police will want to speak with you, Sydney."

"Me? Why me? I had nothing to do with it."

She tasted the brew, and then set down the cup. "Do you have an alibi?"

"For Christ's sake, Deidre, I didn't kill Meri."

"Without an alibi, Sydney, you're toast."

"Damn it, Deidre!" He strode into the kitchen. "Are you certain it was Meri?"

The blind woman nodded.

"That bastard," he muttered.

"Are we talking bastards, in general, Sydney? One of your relatives? Or was your comment self-incriminating?"

"My loving wife," he gritted.

"The police must be wondering about the killer. I know I am." She wet her lips, twice. "It was you, wasn't it, Sydney?"

His eyes widened in shock. "What happened to love, honor and cherish?"

"You tell me, Sydney."

"Deidre, I can't get involved in a murder investigation."

"Hard to avoid, considering last night."

"Last night?"

"You went out, Sydney."

"No, I didn't."

"Yes you did. When Meri was being murdered, you were out. What's worse, when you got home you refused to tell me where you'd been." She smiled blindly. "To me, that means you killed her."

"Stop thinking!"

"Where were you?"

"I went for a walk."

"If you went for a walk, how did you get covered in perfume?"

"Perfume?"

"You reeked of it when you got into bed."

"It must've been your perfume. You know how you wear perfume, to bed."

"No, Sydney. It wasn't my scent." She nibbled her lower lip waiting for him to comment. When her husband said nothing she continued with, "It was hers, wasn't it? It was Meri's. You were with her."

"No! Wait. I remember, now. I stopped for a drink at a bar. It was crowded. I sat next to a woman who was oozing perfume. Perfume oozes, Deidre. It oozes into places you would not believe. Ask anybody."

"Any married man, you mean?"

Popovitch was silent for some time. In due course he said, "I suppose you told Vasiliev about me being out?"

"I'm sorry, Sydney. Serge and I were discussing possible candidates for Meri's killer, and I may have mentioned your name."

His arms rose and fell. "My life gets better and better."

"You have to go to the police, Sydney."

"If I go to the police, they'll arrest me for killing Meri."

"Not if you didn't do it."

"You don't believe that. They won't either."

"Use your head, Sydney." The tip of her pink tongue skidded across her lips. "The police will track Meri's calls. Those will lead to you. They'll wonder why you didn't come forward." Deidre shrugged her shoulders. "Everyone will wonder."

"But, I didn't kill her."

"You were with Meri Darling, last night."

Popovitch dragged his hands across his face.

"Fine. Fine. I was with Meri. We talked. She was alive when I left. End of story."

"Hardly the end, Sydney. The woman was murdered."

Popovitch heaved in a breath. "Harry Steiner."

The blind woman frowned. Then she asked, "What's a hairy steiner?"

"Steiner's a rapist. He's a killer. He's an escapee from an insane asylum. Harry Steiner's a freak with a foil cap fitted with blinking lights. He killed Meri Darling. He sees an invisible guy named Leon."

"Friend or relation?"

"Will you be serious?"

"Okay. Was the doll the motive for Meri's murder?"

Popovitch touched his mouth with trembling fingertips, and eyed the hallway toward the bedroom. "Forget about that damn doll."

"The police are going to find out about it, Sydney. You may as well tell me its significance."

"How are they going to find out?"

"I'm going to tell them."

"Fine. Fine. Make my life a misery, as if you haven't." He clawed at his hair, in frustration. "Meri and I sort of stole the doll from Steiner."

Deidre blindly squinted. "How does one 'sort of' steal?'"

"All right, damn you, we stole it."

"So, Mr. Steiner killed Meri Darling trying to retrieve his own property?"

"He'd have killed Meri for the pleasure of it, doll or not."

"But, if Mr. Steiner killed Meri why did he leave her body in our neighborhood? Why not in his neighborhood? Why not in somebody else's neighborhood?"

"Because that lunatic wanted to scare me."

"Are you gambling, again, Sydney?" Deidre raised her eyebrows. "Did you borrow money from Mr. Steiner?"

"I tell you a mental case who rapes and murders killed Meri Darling and the only concerns you have are about my gambling?"

"How do you know Mr. Steiner did it? Were you there? Did you help?"

"What do you take me for?"

The blind woman took another sip of tea, listening to her husband's nervous footfalls. Eventually she said, "Was I such a bad wife, Sydney?"

He stopped, his back to her, but said nothing.

"I'm sorry for making your life a misery," she said. "I didn't mean to. Was it the sex? Mr. Vasiliev says that sexual spontaneity is critical to a happy marriage."

Her husband remained silent.

"Would it have helped if I'd been blessed with an innate desire for whips?" she asked.

His face took on a bewildered expression as he turned toward her. "Whips?"

"I'm willing to forgive and forget, Sydney." She raised the cup and drank more tea. Then she returned the cup to the table. "But, we have to tell the police about Mr. Steiner. We have to let the police about your affair with Meri Darling."

Popovitch fanned the air in front of his waist. "No way am I doing that."

"I'm not giving you a choice."

"You're going to get me killed!"

"We have to do the right thing."

"If I implicate Steiner in her murder, I'll implicate myself."

"How?"

"Meri and I worked for Steiner."

"Why would you work for a murder-rapist, Sydney? Surely there must've been other jobs? Say, like helping an embezzler? Or assisting a bank robber?"

"I didn't know anything about Steiner until Meri told me!"

Deidre fell silent, composing herself. Then she asked, "Meri Darling was having sex with Mr. Steiner while she was having an affair with you, while I was getting nothing?"

"Fine. Fine. Keep twisting the knife in my back."

"What did Meri give you that I didn't?"

"It doesn't matter."

"I guess, for once, you're right." Mrs. Popovitch smiled at nothing. "Shall I telephone the police? Or, will you?"

"There's got to be another way."

"There isn't."

"They'll grill me for hours. My name will be misspelled in every newspaper." Popovitch looked over at her, his face bleak. "The whole world will think I'm a sexual degenerate."

"Not unless I'm forced to discuss your sexual history."

Popovitch went into the kitchen, leaned against the counter next to the stove and watched his wife for a long moment. "Just this once, can't you help me?"

"You told me that you'd given Meri the doll."

"I did."

"Surely Meri would've given it to Mr. Steiner to avoid being killed?"

"Handing over the doll wouldn't have saved her."

"Okay. But, Mr. Steiner wouldn't have been stupid enough to kill her without getting the doll. Right?"

"You don't know Steiner."

The blind woman's voice became higher pitched. "So, if Mr. Steiner has the doll why did he try to frighten you by leaving Meri's body just down the block?"

"Fine. Fine. Don't believe me. Maybe you can help them strap me onto the death-house gurney?"

Her brows arched, expectantly. "Would they let me do that?"

"Whatever it takes to make you happy." Popovitch's chin dropped to his chest, his large hands clenched into fists.

"Don't kid yourself, Sydney. Happiness is something forever lost to me."

"Well, maybe this will help. I'll be going with you to Hull." Popovitch raised his eyes to his wife. They were cold, dark hollows. "I'm going to make this trip unforgettable—for both of us."

Chapter 6
"Interrupted Song and Dance"

Shortly after noon, across from 5 Derne Street and down half a block, Steiner's van pulled to a stop. Black curtains blocked its side and rear windows. One of the roadside tires had a whitewall. As the engine's rpm's dropped to an idle, a cloud of gray smoke belched from the exhaust pipe and circled lazily upward, disappearing into a cold blue sky.

Steiner huddled behind the steering wheel. Tio Menotti and Mike Zeeman occupied one side of the dining booth. A deck of cards, several beer cans, and an ashtray, a pack of cigarettes, a lighter and a smattering of cash littered the tabletop.

"Hey, Creep," Tio said. "How 'bout you and your invisible pal, Leon, sit in for another game?"

"Leon ain't invisible, Menotti."

"You hear that, Baby?"

"I heard, Tio. I don't believe."

"What about the game, Creep?"

"You fuckers cheated." Steiner looked at the empty passenger seat. "Back off, Leon! You know damn well those bastards cheated."

Menotti and Zeeman wore dark suits and topcoats. Steiner was dressed as before, the lights on his foil headgear blinking sporadically.

"You hear that, Baby? We cheat."

"Yeah, Tio. And, now, the Creep won't play with us."

"You think the Creep and Leon play with themselves?"

Zeeman grinned at his partner. "No surprises there, Tio."

Zeeman shuffled the cards back and forth. Menotti puffed on the cigar that smoldered at one corner of his mouth. Steiner left the van's driver seat. The little man walked back to the booth and settled into it, opposite the partners. From the fresh bruise on Steiner's chin and oozing cut over his left eye, he looked like he had been in a brawl and lost the battle to all concerned.

"When do we make our move, Bad Man?" Zeeman asked.

"Yeah, Creep," chimed Menotti. "You been stalling all morning."

"We move when I say we move," Steiner snapped. Then he glanced over one shoulder. "No more shit, Leon! This is my gig. I call the shots."

There were seconds of silence as Steiner tilted toward the side window, and pulled the curtain away to peek out.

"I'm told that doll's stuffed with Bling-blings, Bad Man," Zeeman remarked. "An unregistered cool million."

"Seems like you forgot to tell us that," the Menotti chimed.

Steiner jerked back, letting the curtain drop. Saliva dribbled from one corner of his mouth.

"Nobody's s'posed to know," the little man said. Then he twisted to look toward the rear of the van. "You been jaw-flappin' again, Leon?"

Menotti took a deep breath, and let it out. His words barely audible, he stiffly said, "End of my tether, Baby."

"Keep to the plan, Tio." Zeeman's dark brows arched as he returned his attention to the little man. "Where'd you get the scratch to cover a million dollar load, Bad Man?"

"None of your fuckin' business."

"I get the feelin' there's a lot to this gig that you haven't told us," Menotti told Steiner.

"Tio's making a good point, Bad Man."

"Nikolay Kandinsky, Creep. You wouldn't be working for him, would you?"

"Up yours!" Steiner snapped. "Both of you."

The little man jerked aside the curtain and resumed looking outside.

"You shoulda' told us about the Russian, Creep." A momentary flex of jaw muscles rippled across Menotti's face. "Him being in the game changes the score. Me and Baby don't like when the score changes."

"Relax, Menotti," Steiner snorted, still staring outside. "As soon as Blind Lady leaves, it'll be dance time. You and Mr. Zeeman will do your job and be on your way."

"If the doll's there," added Zeeman.

A series of cars and trucks rumbled past.

"What if the doll ain't in there, Creep?" Menotti said. "You and Leon ever consider that?"

"It's there, Menotti."

The burly man pulled the cigar from his mouth and blew a plume of smoke toward the little man. "What if them Bling-blings ain't in it? Did you think of that?"

Zeeman chimed in with, "I'd think that'd piss off Kandinsky."

"They're there."

"Who says?" Menotti asked.

"I do."

"You told us the doll wasn't in Popovitch's flat when you searched, Bad Man."

"Relax, Mr. Zeeman. I got the action covered."

"The point is, what makes you think it would be there, now?"

"Sydney-Boy keeps the doll with him. Takes it everywhere he goes."

"A twenty-some inch doll?" Menotti scoffed. "Get real, Creep. No guy does walks around carrying a doll."

"I know what I'm talkin' 'bout, Menotti."

"Popovitch could've shipped it somewhere, Bad Man."

Steiner, still looking outside, gave his head a brief wag. The movement sent the aluminum foil spinning back and forth.

"Sydney-Boy ain't got no friends, Mr. Zeeman."

"Family comes to mind." Menotti blew another stream of smoke at the little man. "But, you didn't consider that." A ghost of a smile crossed the burly man's mug. "Then you wouldn't, because you killed your family."

"The only relation Sydney-Boy's got is his old man, Menotti. Pop's senile. You don't ship important shit to a guy who's senile." Steiner dropped the curtain and twisted toward the partners. "Get this, and get it good." The little man's face became purple with rage; his eyes protruding. "I hired you fuckers to get the doll. That means' you do your job and there's no discussion 'bout anything."

"You didn't tell us about Kandinsky, Creep."

"We have a deal!"

"Let it go, Tio." Zeeman studied Steiner not unlike a hungry cat might peruse the meal-potential of a fat mouse. "Bad Man's right. We cut a deal. Now we've got to see it through."

"Baby, I'm choking, here."

"Stick to the plan, remember?"

Steiner abruptly shrieked, "You don't hand me shit, Leon." He thrust a finger toward the rear of the van. "You don't say shit, about shit, 'lessen I tell you to say shit."

"I'm rememberin' the plan, Baby," Menotti whispered. "But, between him and Leon, followin' our plan ain't getting any easier."

The little man pulled back the curtain, and resumed staring outside.

"His time is coming, Tio." Zeeman sounded confident.

"Baby, I'm tellin' ya we don't need him."

"Only if everything's as Bad Man claims. With a million on the come, let's play it safe."

A bright flush spread from Menotti's neck to his cheeks. "But, when this thing is over, I get him; right?"

"He'll be all yours."

Car brakes squealed.

"Taxi," the little man hissed. He lowered the curtain a moment and tossed a grin toward the rear of the van. "Told you, Leon. You didn't believe. But there it is. Big, yellow taxi." Steiner resumed his voyeuristic pursuit, excitement quivering his voice. "Nearly dance time, gentlemen."

"Got your dance shoes, Baby?"

"Already tapping my toes, Tio."

Steiner suddenly snapped his fingers. The friction of thumb against middle digit released a high, squeaking sound rather than the typical crisp crack.

"Did you hear that, Baby? The Creep's fingers cut a fart."

"Give the man credit, Tio. It's his only talent."

"Bingo." Steiner giggled, still staring out the window. "They're on the move. Sydney-Boy. Blind Lady." He made an obscene noise with his tongue. "Look at the bouncin' tits on that bitch!"

Menotti looked over at his partner, his face going grim. "I don't like what I'm hearin' baby."

"The plan will take care of him, Tio."

"The suitcases!" Steiner continued, excitedly. "Nothin' like a fuckin' deal comin' together." The little man pulled back from the window and glared toward the rear of the van. "No kibitzin' when my dick's jumpin', Leon. This was all my plan." The little man went back to looking outside. "Look at that bitch's ass. Those cheeks could crack walnuts." One hand went up and stroked the aluminum foil cap, his dark eyes beaming with lust. "Warm up your knuckles, gentlemen. Time to crack out the Popovitch beat."

"I'm certainly gonna' crack out somethin', Creep."

Zeeman slipped the deck of cards into his coat pocket. Menotti picked up the cash, and snuffed out his cigar in the ashtray.

"Fuck!" Steiner blurted.

The burly man snorted, "That *definitely* ain't in the runnin', Creep."

"They're *both* gettin' into the cab!"

"You hear that, Baby?"

"Bad Man's been outsmarted."

Steiner dropped the curtain. "You're ridin' shotgun, Leon!" The little man scrambled out of the booth, and in three frantic strides was back in the driver's seat. "Fasten your seatbelt, Leon! They're makin' a run for it."

As the taxi roared away, Steiner put the van into gear. The weary vehicle jerked forward, falling into line behind the cab.

"You're following too close, Creep."

"Did I ask for your fuckin' advice, Menotti?"

"The Cabbie'll spot you. He'll let Popovitch know. We'll be chasing that doll all over Massachusetts."

"Tio knows what he's talking about, Bad Man. Leave some space."

"I know what I'm doing." Steiner thrust a finger toward the passenger seat. "Do you have a driving license, Leon? Then shut the fuck up!"

"Mrs. Popovitch is blind," Zeeman persisted. "Sydney's probably going along to make sure she gets safely on the ferry."

"'Probably' don't cut shit."

The tall man clenched his fists, his knuckles white.

"You thinking of reworking the plan, Baby?" Menotti snickered.

"Listen up, Bad Man. We could shortcut this gig by going back to their apartment for a search."

"Sydney-Boy ain't getting' outa' my sight." Steiner's hands worked the steering wheel, his eyes locked upon the speeding taxi. "That fuckin' bastard's played me for the last time." His head twisted, momentarily, toward the passenger side. His voice rose high and sharp with anger. "Get your head outa' your ass, Leon! There's nothin' wrong with my drivin'."

"They're changing lanes, Creep."

"I ain't blind, Menotti!"

"Then why are you driving like it?"

Forty minutes later, the taxi pulled to the curb in front of Long Wharf. Steiner drove past to a loading zone, and then stopped at the curb.

"Get the fuck out and follow 'em," Steiner ordered. Then he twisted in the seat toward the passenger side. "Back off, Leon! Or I'll shove my foot up your ass!"

Zeeman stared at Steiner without responding, the muscles in his face flexing.

"Stick with the plan, Baby, remember?"

"I'm beginning to see the problem from your side, Tio."

"He's still mine, remember."

"He's yours, Tio."

"Hey, Creep," said Menotti. "While we're enjoying a stroll near the wharf, what'll you be doing?"

"I'll park this heap. Then Leon and me'll meet you inside."

"Don't be long, Bad Man," Zeeman said, through clenched teeth. "That ferry won't wait."

"Just keep Sydney-Boy in sight." Steiner ran tense fingers across the top of his aluminum foil cap. "That's what I'm payin' you fuckers for."

"Tailing Popovitch wasn't the deal, Creep."

"The deal's changed!"

Menotti and Zeeman climbed out of the van onto the sidewalk. As it roared away, the two men headed in the direction of the terminal building.

"You see what I mean about the Creep?"

"Could be he won't make it to Hull if we corner Popovitch on the ferry."

"He's mine, remember? That means if there's tossing overboard to be done, I get to do it."

Zeeman grinned at his partner. "You've always been a party animal."

They continued along the sidewalk in silence for ten yards. As they neared a newspaper kiosk, the headlines caught Menotti's eyes:

Woman Strangled in Beacon Hill. He stopped, shoved in coins, then
he took out one of the publications.

"Since when do you patronize the fourth estate?" Zeeman
stopped next to his partner.

"Beacon Hill don't get many murders."

The two men moved off, while the burly man scanned the lead
article. Suddenly his feet locked to the cement.

"Baby, this can't be."

Zeeman's ceased his stride. "What?"

"Meri's dead!"

"What happened?"

"Strangled."

Zeeman breathed in and out rapidly, his mind trying to deny
what he had heard. "I was with her just last night."

"I'm reading it right here." Menotti shook the newspaper. "No
mistake. The cops identified her fingerprints."

Zeeman grabbed the newspaper. "Any arrests?"

"Not yet. But, you can bet your ass the cops are looking for us."
Menotti glanced around, his eyes suddenly wide with worry. "I told
you we shouldn't have threatened her."

"Should've, would've, could've. They don't count, Tio."
Zeeman turned pages, and resumed reading. "No witnesses."

"BOLO?"

"One issued for you and me."

"Well, I guess that's clear enough."

"Yeah."

"Let's hit the bricks, Baby."

Zeeman folded the newspaper, and shoved it into his coat
pocket. "Just as soon as we get the doll."

"Who do you think killed her?"

Zeeman heaved his broad shoulders. "Meri didn't have a lot of
friends."

"I'm thinkin' it was the Creep," said Menotti.

"I don't see how. Meri'd checked out of her hotel and was
waiting on what to do, until he talked to me. She was supposed to
head for Hull first ferry this morning."

"The Creep must've followed you."

"Bad Man didn't know I was going anywhere."

"He could've followed us home. Staked out the place. Then when you left, he followed."

"Bad Man's paranoid. But he's not going to spend his nights watching our windows."

Menotti looked toward the parking area. "I don't see the Creep's van."

"Bad Man couldn't find his ass with both hands. So, a parking place might take a while."

"Baby, I don't see him driving around."

"Tio, even if Bad Man was watching our place, I took a taxi. I kept an eye out the rear window. Nobody followed."

The burly man returned his gaze to his partner. "Then somebody tipped him."

"Who? Bad Man's not loved or admired."

"Popovitch. Meri might've called him. You know. Asked him to meet."

"To do what?"

"I don't know. Maybe to discuss killing Blind Lady. Or, whatever."

The partners moved on.

"I don't see Popovitch with a motive for killing Meri."

"Maybe the Creep got to him. You know. The doll changed hands. The Creep agreed to back off if Popovitch pointed him to Meri."

Zeeman glanced toward the parking lot. "Leaving us chasing air?"

"It would explain why the Creep's van is nowhere in sight."

Ahead, a Red Cap loaded the Popovitch's luggage onto a cart.

"Tio, you don't kill the one you hired to kill your wife. It's bad for collecting the insurance."

"That a rule, Baby?"

"Pretty much universally honored."

"Where'd you and Meri hook up?" Menotti asked.

"A rib joint called the Silk Road," Zeeman replied. "It's in the Financial District."

"You'd have noticed the Creep's wreck driving in that area."

"But, I didn't see it."

"Kandinsky could've put a hit on her." Menotti walked stride for stride with Zeeman.

"I don't think so. If the Russian was behind her death his people would've taken out Popovitch and Bad Man, to clean the slate."

"Which brings us back to Bad Man as her killer," Zeeman muttered, his eyes returning to the parking area. "Still no van."

Moments passed as they continued side by side.

"Okay," Menotti said. "Let's figure it was the Creep. He must've spotted Meri by accident. It happens."

"Not often. Not with her changing hotels every week."

"Baby, you keep shooting down my ideas."

A tour bus rolled past, lots of lost faces stared out the side windows.

"You read what the killer did to her?" Menotti asked.

"I read."

Menotti's face was doughy with emotion, his eyes were red, and sweat gleamed atop his bald head.

"Stripped her, raped her, strangled her, and dumped her body like so much shit." Menotti hesitated. "When we pin down who did it, I'm gonna' take my time killin' him."

"I'll bring popcorn for the show, Tio."

They continued for a few more seconds.

"I've been doing a rethink, Baby."

"About Meri's killer?"

Menotti's chin bobbed. "Insurance or not, I'm still thinking Popovitch."

"I don't see him for it, Tio."

The Red Cap pushed the cart holding the Popovitch's luggage into the terminal building. Popovitch and his wife followed, arm in arm. Menotti and Zeeman resumed their movements.

"Look at them," Zeeman said. "Could you kill her?"

"I could kill him," Menotti returned.

"I'm talking about her."

"No. I couldn't kill her. But that's just me."

"You noticed how she walks?"

"Yeah, Baby, I noticed. Nice walk."

"Just a slight sway. Not sexy. Just enough to make a guy notice."

"Let's get a hustle on," Menotti said. "The Popovitchs are heading toward the ticket counter."

The two men rushed into the building, then slowed their pace to a walk, trailing behind Mr. and Mrs. Popovitch.

"I'll get closer to hear her destination," Zeeman told his partner. "You hang back, keeping an eye on him."

Menotti stopped. Zeeman continued after the couple.

Minutes later, Mr. and Mrs. Popovitch left the ticket counter. Menotti fell in behind them and followed as far as the ferry's boarding gate. A few minutes later, Zeeman caught up with him.

"Hull?" the burly man asked his partner.

"They're both going." Zeeman held up a pair of boarding passes. "We've got a twenty minute boat ride."

"You buy the Creep a ticket?"

"Let him get his own."

The ferry whistle sounded.

"We'd better get on board." Zeeman checked his watch. "If Bad Man doesn't make this one, it'll be an hour to the next ferry."

"How do you want to deal with Popovitch?"

"It'll be safer to wait until we get to Hull."

The two men moved off.

Chapter 7
"A Ferry Ride"

"**I**'m curious, Sydney," Deidre Popovitch said, after getting comfortable in the deck-chair next to her husband. "I mentioned divorce. You countered with a second honeymoon. Now, we're on a ferry to la-la land for the mentally deprived. Was Meri Darling behind this romantic whim?"

"I don't want to talk about her." Sydney's jaw muscles rippled.

"Surely, you spoke to her about me?"

"Considering who Meri and I worked for, we had other things to talk about."

"Nonsense. If she had any feelings for you, I'd be at the forefront of any discussion. Me, and how to get rid of me."

"I'm not talking about Meri."

Popovitch rubbernecked, his eyes going from passenger to passenger. When his vision focused upon Zeeman and Menotti, he paused. They fit the description of Meri's ne'er-do-well cohorts; the pair she had testified against. However, Zeeman and Menotti were supposed to be in prison.

"So, this unexpected flash of renewed romance is on the level?" she asked.

"I'm trying to make amends, okay?"

"Far be it from me to complain, Sydney." A mocking smile touched her face. "A second honeymoon beats the hell out of homicide."

"Will you forget what Vasiliev told you?"

"Serge isn't a liar, Sydney." Her smile flickered to a frown. "And romantic impulses aren't you."

"What am I, Deidre?"

"A narcissist."

Popovitch looked over at his wife in frustration. "I'm a self-involved mental maniac?"

"If it quacks like a duck and walks like a duck..." She shrugged. "What can I say, Sydney?"

"Fine. Fine. I get it. All I do is think of myself."

Deidre sat in silence for a while her ears cocked, listening carefully. Then the blind woman splayed her hands, matter-of-factly.

"Why now, Sydney?"

"Why now, what?" he returned, impatiently.

"Why are we taking a second honeymoon now? Why not a month ago. Or, a month from now? What makes this moment in time your choice for revitalizing our dying marriage?"

"A month ago my father's bed and breakfast was fully booked," her husband answered, without hesitation. "Considering my huge mistake with the door last year, I thought it would be safer to wait until the tourist season was over. This was the first weekend Pop had no reservations."

"Very thoughtful," she returned, dryly.

"You don't believe me?"

"Don't take it so hard, Sydney. With my corpse worth a fortune, I have to consider possibilities."

Popovitch weighed his answer carefully. "I made a mistake. I should have told you about the insurance." Shadows of guilt filled her husband's face. "Why can't you let it drop?"

"Two million dollars. A double indemnity clause in the event of homicide. Why would you purchase a policy with such specific terms?"

"Since it bothers you, I'll cancel it."

"You've already renewed it to run another term."

He gave his wife a sharp, surprised look. "Did Vasiliev tell you that?"

"No. The insurance agent did." She tilted back and crossed her legs. "Tell me something, Sydney. Should I die in the midst of unpleasantness, during this not-so-nice outing, would you feel an unbearable loss? Or will your grief be assuaged by the insurance proceeds?"

Her husband let go a hollow laugh. "Forget about the insurance."

"I can't, Sydney."

Popovitch pushed his fingers through his hair, dragging it back from his brow. "Could you, at least, try?"

"Tell me something, Sydney. Why did Meri's death change your mind about accompanying me to Hull?"

"I don't understand."

"Your contract with Allied. How did her dying cancel it?"

His face pinched with irritation. "It didn't. I'm... I'm here to protect you."

"Protect me?"

"Steiner left Meri's body nearby as a message. He can't take on me without Kandinsky's help, so he's coming after you. That's why I'm going along."

"My protector." There was a flash of her white teeth. "But, what makes you think that Mr. Steiner will go to Hull? He doesn't know about our trip—unless you told him."

He tossed his wife an irritated glance. "Why would I tell Steiner?"

"Why would you insure my life for two million?"

He leaned back, crossed his legs and extended one arm across the back of the adjacent chair. "Give it a rest, okay?"

"It's the amount that bothers me, Sydney." Deidre brushed at the hem of her skirt, pulling it modestly across her knees. "I'm having difficulties justifying the need for such a huge amount, unless you plan to kill me."

"The policy won't be honored if I'm suspected in your murder."

"But, you wouldn't have been a suspect. Meri Darling was supposed to arrive a day ahead of time, wait for me to arrive and then kill me while you were in Boston, creating a rock-solid alibi."

"Who told you that? Vasiliev? Has he tapped our phones?"

"How I came by the information is moot, Sydney." Deidre's head moved fractionally from side to side. "The point is, I know that's what you had planned."

"Don't be ridiculous."

"Am I?"

"Deidre, you can't have it both ways. Either I killed Meri, or I hired her to kill you. Which is it?"

She dipped and raised his chin slightly. "I'm impressed by your analysis, Sydney. Frankly, it makes me question why you were last in your graduating class."

"Let's say that I was crazy enough to want you dead," he went on, hoping to press his point home.

"Yes, let's."

A snappy retort rose to Popovitch's tongue, but he bit it back. "How would I convince Meri to do the killing?"

"If anybody could, Sydney, it'd be you."

Popovitch shifted in the chair, her words making him uncomfortable. "You didn't know Meri Darling."

"Mr. Vasiliev says a woman in love will do anything, for the object of her affection."

"That damn Russian is killing our marriage." Popovitch gritted the words between his teeth. "You do know that?"

The ferry engines rumbled in the background. Passenger footsteps ambled past. Seawater lapped and splashed against the vessel's hull.

Eventually Deidre said, "The trouble with blind travel is the inability to see new surroundings."

"Now, it's my fault you're blind?"

"Of course not, Sydney. I'm merely stating a fact." The ghost of a smile brightened her face for a moment. "I'm actually delighted with our adventure. My disappointment is that my excitement must be limited to smells and sounds."

"Sounds like I finally did something right."

A number of passengers ambled past, heading into the salon for a drink. One of them staggered and bumped into Deidre before continuing on.

The blind woman wrinkled her nose. "Did a fish with a leaking bladder try to trample me?"

"Fish don't walk or wear tweed or smoke pipes."

"Dare I hope that it and its failing organs swam onward?"

"Your nostrils are safe for the time being."

With her free hand, she did a brief fan of the air in front of her face. "You're certain your father is expecting just us this weekend?"

"Everything's arranged."

"You spoke to your father, not Charlie Owens?"

"I talked to Pop, okay?"

"I'm curious, Sydney." Mrs. Popovitch turned toward his voice, offering her husband a wry, twisted smile. "When you speak to your father, do you ever inquire as to his health?"

"He's fine."

"But do you actually ask him?"

"I don't have to. Pop's always fine."

"Poor Sydney. Always on the outside looking in."

The muscles around Popovitch's jaw flexed, thickening his neck with renewed aggravation. He turned toward her. "What's that supposed to mean?"

"People like being asked about their health, Sydney. It's a small thing. Admittedly, it's a waste of time from any honest perspective. We really don't want to hear about it, good or bad." Deidre grimaced and then forced a momentary grin. "In some cases we might actually hope the person we've queried is doing ill. Nevertheless, asking people makes them feel special. That's a nice thing to do, Sydney."

"My father's old, Deidre. He's bonkers. Half the time he doesn't know how he feels or who he is. There's not much point in asking him anything."

"Why don't you admit it, Sydney? You're completely devoid of social skills."

"Fine. Fine. I get it," he seethed, looking away. "I'm not sensitive to other people's feelings. When I get home I'll take a flier at self-improvement."

"It would be a waste of time."

"You've become an expert on emotional limitations?"

"Everyone tries to improve, Sydney. The trouble is, no one ever does." An amused smirk twisted her beautiful face. "Every night, the entire world goes to bed praying to receive perfection by morning. Unfortunately, sunrise occurs and everyone awakens unchanged." Her hands rose and then fell back to her lap. "For most people this nightly grind is a mild disappointment. Something to mull over between coffee sips, and nibbles on a prune Danish." Her dark hair slid back and forth across her shoulders. "But for you, Sydney, every morning must be an absolute catastrophe."

He shot her an angry look at his wife. "Why is it that ninety-nine percent of our conversations lead to arguments?"

"Are we about to argue?"

"I think it's very likely, unless you change the subject."

"All right, why don't we talk about Meri Darling? A popular topic, I'm sure, for a man of meandering morals."

"I told you…"

"Of course you did, Sydney," the blind woman cut in. "You often tell me things. But, in each case you lie."

Popovitch raised his fists to shoulder level, then dropped back to the chair arms. "I don't know why I bother."

"I don't know why you do, either, Sydney. You're the world's worst liar. But, you are an excellent womanizer." Deidre made a momentary finger-thrust at nothing. "There, you see? One fine example of your peculiar brand of success, and I complimented you on it."

"I'm a damn good systems analyst."

"Sydney, your last four projects were busts."

"It was not my fault those contracts were cancelled. So, stop trying to put me on a guilt trip."

"I'd never dream of trying to do so, Sydney. Guilt has never been part of your emotional repertoire."

Her husband's fuming irritation showed as he muttered, "Did your mother never tell you to keep quiet if you couldn't say anything good about someone?"

"Frequently." Deidre shifted her shoulders up and down. "But, if I'd followed her advice I'd never have spoken to you after the close of our honeymoon."

"Fine. Fine. Keep hacking away. You were always fond of an emotional bloodletting"

The blind woman crossed her arms, her head tilted down slightly. "While you were in the shower this morning, your father telephoned."

"Did you ask about his health?" he taunted.

"Absolutely. And Pop inquired about mine." She paused a beat, smiling secretly. "That's what people with normal social skills do, Sydney."

"Enjoy it while you can, Deidre."

"Pop said to tell you that your friend did not arrive yesterday." Her voice quivered with sudden anger. "He wanted to know if he should continue to hold her reservation." The blind woman cocked the ear nearest her husband, awaiting his response. "Who's your friend, Sydney?"

Popovitch's chin hit his chest. "Pop's mistaken, okay?" His head came up his eyes clenched shut. "He's senile." His eyes opened and he let out a long sigh. "Senile men make a lot of mistakes."

"They certainly do. But, in this case your father's sagging mental faculties conjured up Meri Darling's name." A ghost of a smile moved her lips. "Since we both know that she was a very good friend of yours, why was she attending our second honeymoon if not to murder me?"

His hands gave the chair-arms a white-knuckled squeeze. "You're twisting what he said out of context."

"How so?"

"Obviously, my old man read about Meri's murder and got things mixed up."

"Including her reservation?"

Her husband's broad shoulders dipped, slightly; his head still turning, his eyes still wandering among the passengers. "Can we finish the ferry-ride without further chit-chat?"

"Wouldn't you find it tedious?"

"It would be a blessing."

"You know how much I love to please, Sydney. But, I'm not sure your request is practical." An angry smile curled the corners of Deidre's lips. "Silence could become a habit. That, in turn, could lead to emotional stagnation. You'd become a model husband. I'd become your obedient slave." Her feet shuffled on the deck. "Frankly, Sydney, I'm not sure our fragile marriage would survive such a serious remodeling."

"Zip it, damn you!"

The blind woman gave an empty little laugh. "People who are very good at verbal abuse, like us, expect to receive it—nay, look forward to it. Should it cease—well, it's like sex without foreplay. You reach the expected result. But the trip's not nearly as fun." Deidre wet her lips several times. "Of all your lovers, why did Meri Darling become your long-term choice?"

Popovitch tossed his wife a searing look and then resumed his visual search of the passengers. "I'm done talking."

"I thought men like you enjoyed bragging about their extramarital flings. You know: wink-wink, nudge-nudge."

"Fine. Fine," he gritted. "Open a vein. Let in the snake venom."

"Were you in love with Meri? Or was it strictly physical." Deidre worried her lower lip a moment. "Did she love you? As much as I did when we first married?"

He looked into his wife's beautiful face for a long moment. Then his shoulders moved ever so slightly. "You're twisting the truth, again."

"I'm seeking a straight answer."

A long sigh rushed out of his mouth. "Meri loved only Meri."

"Then why did the two of you become intimates?"

"You can't believe Vasiliev, Deidre. Meri and I were strictly business."

"Sydney, is there a mirror in the ferry's men's room?"

"Probably. Why?"

"I'd like you to go there and gaze into it."

He gave her a bewildered look. "What for?"

"I want to know if your nose growing."

"You're deliberately running me up a wall!"

"Why? Because you're ashamed of your affair with Meri?" The blind woman quickly folded her hands in her lap. "That poor woman is dead. Stop lying about your relationship, with her."

"Fine. Fine. You're right." Popovitch slapped the chair arms with both hands. "I had an affair with Meri. Now, can we move on?"

"She just appeared in your bed?"

Popovitch's hands moved slightly, his head tilting, and his eyes once more scanning. "Meri did not appear in my bed. I invited her. Yes, I feel ashamed. No, I'll never do it again."

"I should think not. Her body must be ice-cold."

"You know what I mean."

"Why did Meri Darling come to our flat the day she died?"

His head revolved toward his wife like a gate in a high wind, his mouth open in shock. "How did you come by that fiction?"

"Meri Darling didn't live in our neighborhood, Sydney. Yet Meri died there."

"Because Steiner brought here body there."

"No way." Deidre raised a finger for emphasis. "She came to our part of town under her own power."

"Is that more of Vasiliev's fiction?"

"If Mr. Steiner killed Meri, as you claim, if he left her in the parking lot in order to scare you, as you claim, wouldn't it have been far more frightening to leave her corpse on our doorstep?"

"Steiner's crazy. Who knows how he thinks?"

"Meri came to our flat while I was visiting Mr. Vasiliev for my Russian lesson." A beat of silence passed. "You were the only one who could've killed her. The only question I has is whether you killed Meri Darling in our apartment or in the parking lot?"

"Get it through you head, Deidre, Meri didn't come to our flat!"

"You're lying, Sydney. I can prove it."

"Fine. Fine." Popovitch ground his teeth, his lips tight. "Yes, Meri came to see me. Steiner had tried to kill her. She was scared. She wanted my help. I gave her advice. She left."

The ferry shuddered as its engines started. Alarmed, both Deidre and Sydney moved their heads, looking around for an explanation. The arguing pair relaxed once the vessel began to move out to sea.

"It doesn't wash," Deidre told her husband.

"I had no reason to kill Meri!"

"Sydney, you're forgetting the doll."

"What has it to do with anything?"

"You told me that Mr. Steiner killed Meri to get the doll."

"That's right."

"But why kill *her* when *you* have the doll?"

"I told you. I gave the doll to Meri."

"Stop it, Sydney."

"I'm not lying!"

"Of course you're lying. You're always lying. It's what you do best." She blindly smoothed the lay of her blouse. "Why's that doll so important, Sydney?"

His face reflected growing defeat. "It's not important."

"I know you, Sydney. You're not going to risk your neck for something unless it's very valuable." Suddenly the blind woman squinted her unseeing eyes. "Is it an antique?"

"If you don't shut your mouth about that damn…"

"What will you do, Sydney? Hit me? A blind woman? In front of all the other passengers?" She leaned back a little. "Go ahead. Take your best shot."

"Why can't you leave anything alone?"

"I'm trying to help you, Sydney."

"Some help."

"The police won't stop digging. Not in a murder case. Not until they find out about everyone and everything involved. It's just a matter of time before they discover your relationship with Meri, with Mr. Steiner. They'll question me, Sydney. I'll tell them about the doll."

He jumped to his feet screaming, "You'll do as I say!"

"Sit down, Sydney. People must be staring at your rudeness." She reached out and patted the arm of his empty chair. "We can't have potential jurors thinking that you're unstable as well as homicidal."

Her husband slumped back into his chair, looking around at staring eyes. "For two cents I'd wring your neck, here and now."

"And lose four million?"

Popovitch dragged his hands across his face.

"Between you and me and the sunshine, Sydney, how much is that doll worth?"

"Fine. Fine. You want to know how much, I'll tell you how much. A million."

"For a doll?"

"It's a special doll."

"For that price, it should be." Deidre twisted toward her husband. Her sightless eyes glowed with interest. "Why would Mr. Steiner invest a million dollars in a doll?" She blinked twice. "Why would anyone? More importantly, where would a man who wears an aluminum foil cap and sees an invisible man named Leon get the money to purchase such a doll?"

Her husband dusted the knees of his jeans. "It doesn't belong to him."

"He stole it before you stole it?"

"He didn't steal it. It just isn't his."

Deidre exhaled slowly and smiled. "Where is the doll, Sydney?"

"It's safe until I can give it to Kandinsky."

The blind woman straightened in her chair, and did another adjustment to her skirt. "Did it belong to the person you've been looking for?"

"How could you possibly think that I've been looking for someone?"

"You've been moving in your seat since we sat down. The ferry isn't new to us, so you're not taking a tourist's interest in your surroundings." Deidre smiled, clearly amused. "You're not one for puppies, or kittens, so I'm assuming that you don't have pin-worms. Therefore, you've been shifting positions to look for someone."

"I'm not looking for anyone." Popovitch sagged back, his breathing ragged. "I'm having trouble getting comfortable." He checked his watch. "Look, there's about five minutes left on this miserable voyage. What say we give me a break and ride it out in silence?"

"No can do, Sydney. I'm feeling far too emotionally traumatized because you know somebody rich enough to own a million dollar doll and I don't."

He looked at her, his eyes cold and unblinking. "Would you like me to introduce you to Nikolay Kandinsky? Because right now I'm in the mood."

"Who is Mr. Kandinsky?"

A Russian mobster. Steiner works for him."

Her voice became breathless. "Sydney, I never dreamed that you'd know a gangster. For the first time since we exchanged vows, you've moved up in my estimation. Congratulations. No longer will I consider you the turd in the milk pail."

"God, please strike her dead."

"Does this make you a mobster? Am I a *mobsterette*?"

"Nikolay Kandinsky is no joking matter, Deidre. He makes Steiner look like a choir boy."

Deidre fell silent, thinking. Then she asked, "Is Mr. Kandinsky following us? Is that who you've been looking for?"

"Him or his men or Steiner, or the two goons Meri used to work with." He hesitated a beat. "You know, I just remembered. Those two clowns threatened to kill her."

"Who?"

"Tio Menotti and Mike Zeeman."

Deidre's lips parted as she drew in a breath. "How do they rank among the choir boys?"

"I wouldn't cross them."

"Why would they want Meri Darling dead?"

"She testified against them. Because of her testimony, they spent three years behind bars. Meri was part of the Badger Game they were running. But she turned State's Evidence and got off Scott free."

Deidre He nodded slowly, moving her hands to the chair arms. "Are Mr. Menotti and Mr. Zeeman in Boston?"

"Meri said they were supposed to serve another six months. But, I'm not so sure."

"Revenge makes for a very good motive."

He looked at her with surprised eyes. "Does that mean you finally believe me about Meri?"

"Right now I'm more concerned with your survival prospects?"

"Me?"

"Is somebody going to kill you? And more to my point of concern, are those persons going to kill me because I'm married to you?"

"As usual, you're cheering me toward oblivion."

Deidre took in a deep breath and let out a jerky little sigh. "Do you realize that having the doll—by having, of course, I mean you having it—we've finally reached millionaire status?"

"Millionaires don't ride ferries."

"Sydney, what makes that doll worth a million dollars?"

"It's not the doll. It's the Bling-blings inside the doll."

"Bling-blings?"

"Street name for faceted diamonds; the unregistered, undeclared type."

Her eyes widened with surprised delight. "Not only have you become a mobster, and a millionaire, but you've gone from being an incompetent computer programmer to an illicit purveyor of illegal diamonds!"

"Keep your voice down."

"I can't wait to tell Mr. Vasilicv. He thinks you're an absolute idiot."

"Yeah, well, I've got a few choice words for that damn Russian."

A frown suddenly shadowed her face. "Sydney, how does one convert a million in Bling-blings into cash?"

"When they belong to Nikolay Kandinsky, it's only done with his approval."

"What I mean is *who* would buy them?"

"Diamond brokers."

"Does Boston have diamond brokers?"

"Nikolay Kandinsky kills people who cross him, Deidre."

She raised a finger and waived it. "Technically, those diamonds are yours and mine."

"Yeah, well, I'd like you to convince Kandinsky of that."

"At this moment, Sydney, those Bling-blings are community property. *Our* community property." She wet her lips. "You can give your half to Mr. Kandinsky. I'm keeping mine."

"No, Deidre, not if you put a gun to my head."

"Possession is nine-tenths of the law, Sydney." She made a display of her hands. "We have. Mr. Kandinsky doesn't." The blind woman let out a sparkling giggle. "I've never been a millionaire, before."

The tone of his voice dropped a notch, the words coming out stiff and spaced. "You're insane."

"Sydney, you shouldn't keep saying that. People might overhear and wonder about me."

Chapter 8
"Hull"

After the ferry docked at Pemberton Point Terminal, Mike Zeeman and Tio Menotti disembarked. They were the last passengers to leave the vessel. Unhurried, the pair moved along the wake of the other arrivals, feigning the role of eager tourists. Each of their steps, however, was measured. The partners purposely stayed a dozen, or so, yards behind so as to avoid observation by Popovitch.

"Two suitcases ain't much for a second honeymoon," Menotti remarked, carefully watching the couple.

"Sydney Popovitch isn't planning a lengthy celebration," Zeeman grimly returned.

Deidre walked next to her husband, her right hand gripping his left elbow. The couple's steps, as they headed in the direction of the taxi-stand, were slow and reluctant, like two soldiers approaching a war zone.

"Popovitch don't know how lucky he is," Menotti said.

"You don't have to sell me."

In spite of his size and fitness, Popovitch struggled with the couple's luggage. He held the large case in his right hand; the small suitcase balanced atop the first, his upper arm holding it in place. His head continually moved back and forth as if fearful of what he might see, or who might see him.

"I'm thinking Popovitch changed his mind 'bout killing her," Menotti suggested.

"Not a chance. Meri said that he'd been paying insurance premiums for over a year." Zeeman gave a determined wag to his dark head. "A man doesn't invest that much and then change his mind."

Zeeman had grown up fast and hard. Even as a child, the tall man had wrapped a protective shell around his heart. It did not matter to him how people lived, or died. Man, woman, child—from his perspective each was little more than a manikin. Women to be used. Men to be abused. Children to be ignored. But for reasons

Zeeman could not fathom, Deidre was different. It wasn't pity he felt for her. She was special. From the moment Zeeman had first seen the blind woman, she had touched his heart, she had made him want to protect her. She had made him want to mend his ways.

"They talked during the trip." Menotti's lips pulled back off his teeth. "We both saw how they talked. I'm tellin' ya, Baby, he's changed his mind."

Menotti enjoyed the sunlight reflecting from Mrs. Popovitch's dark hair as she and her husband moved toward a taxi stand. It gave the blind woman's coiffeur the look of molten basalt. Her movements made that liquid-like illusion ebb and flow down her back in the most tantalizing manner.

"Tio, Blind Lady talked. Popovitch merely listened and rankled."

"I didn't see no rankling."

"You were too busy eying her legs."

"Baby, that ain't my fault. She's got them kind of legs." Menotti made a beseeching display of his hands. "You know. Where a guy can't take his eyes off."

"I'm with you, Tio." Zeeman grinned.

"She's seductive. You know them types." Menotti made a small, self-conscious movement. "The ones that get a guy all confused with short skirts."

"She wasn't wearing a short skirt."

"She could've been."

The flow of foot traffic continued for nearly a minute, the partners walking in silence. The other passengers were chatting, excitedly.

Suddenly, Menotti eyed his partner askance. "Baby, you ain't makin' romance plans, are ya?"

Zeeman gave his dark head a hesitant shake.

"Not that Blind Lady wouldn't be heavenly. I get you on that."

"This is business."

Menotti turned up his coat collar, against the cold. "It's just that you ain't sounded the same, since you got a look at her."

"I said, it's business."

Menotti, hesitated, reluctant to continue but unable to stop. "All's I'm sayin' is, this gig is complicated enough without you goin' off the deep end in the romance department."

"Not going to happen."

The Popovitchs continued toward a taxi stand.

The partners separated momentarily, veering around a fat man headed toward the ferry, and then resumed their side-by-side treading.

"I did a rethink," Menotti remarked.

"You're always doing a rethink."

"I'm thinking Popovitch killed Meri."

"I'll bite."

"I'm thinking he realized that Meri wasn't goin' through with the killing, and shut her up."

"I'm not so sure, Tio."

The partners wove in and out of an approaching throng.

"If he did it," Menotti said after pairing up with Zeeman, "I'm takin' my time killin' him. I want the bastard to understand just how big a mistake he made, killing Meri."

"I'm with you, Tio. But, I want to be sure before we act."

"He'll tell us. I'll make sure he tells us."

Zeeman put his hands in his pockets and let his eyes drift. He was curious about who or what was making Popovitch wary. But no threats leaped out. The police were absent. Staring onlookers were nowhere in sight. He saw only a bevy of passengers moving away from the ferry, customers heading toward it.

"Check it out, Baby. Popovitch is rubbernecking like a man workin' a kink."

"He doesn't like being seen with her."

"Then, he's the one who's blind."

"It isn't shame, Tio." Zeeman compressed his lips. "Popovitch is scared."

"Of what? He outweighs her by sixty pounds."

"He knows what he's got to do." The tall man wrinkled his nose against the cold. "He's scared that somebody might be reading his mind."

"Looks to me like he's a man half way up the gallows' stairs."

"He knows he'll be executed if he doesn't pull off the perfect killing. He also knows that he's got only one chance to get it right."

"Which explains why he's lookin' for something to plug his asshole."

Zeeman gave his partner a confused look. "Come again?"

"His brown-eye can't keep its pucker."

"That's a problem, is it?"

"The worst." The burly man let his eyes scan from horizon to horizon. Then, he refocused upon Popovitch. "What if the doll ain't here?"

"It's here. The one thing Bad Man has right is figuring that Popovitch wouldn't travel without it."

"But what if it ain't?"

The tall man's expression hardened. "Then Popovitch will tell us where it is."

"We'll have to find a spot to work on him. Someplace out of the way."

"I heard the Popovitchs talking when they were buying their tickets. The bed and breakfast has cabins."

"Then we'll have a place to gag him, drag him and go to work."

The tall man nodded, his eyes on the couple. He like the way Deidre walked: the slight sway to her hips, the straightness of her back. He liked her smile. He liked the darkness in her eyes. He liked the shape of her calves and ankles. He liked everything about her.

Menotti jutted his chin toward the Popovitchs. "I should've brought my blowtorch."

"What for?"

"Ain't you never heard the expression: 'Hold his feet to the fire'?"

Zeeman considered for a moment. "I don't think we'll need that, Tio."

When the two men neared the taxi stand they stopped, making a point of ignoring the Popovitchs. Popovitch set down the suitcases. Then he and Deidre traded words for a few moments.

"See?" said Menotti, smiling with satisfaction. "They're talkin'. I'm telling ya, Baby, she's got him wrapped around her little finger."

Abruptly Popovitch turned and stalked away.

"The bastard's making a run for it!" Menotti growled.

"Popovitch left the suitcases, with her. So if he's going, the doll isn't along for the ride."

Popovitch stopped when he was about fifty feet from Deidre. He took out his cellular phone, punched numbers and then waited for a connection.

"Who's he talking to?" Menotti demanded.

"I'm not a mind reader, Tio."

"The bastard's hiring someone to make the hit."

"What happened to her having him wrapped around her finger?" Zeeman focused his stare upon Deidre. "She's got her phone out, too."

"They get to this pit-town, and then they both make phone calls." Menotti looked at his partner. "You think they're talking to each other?"

"While you give your brain a rest, Tio, I'll head over to Blind Lady and eavesdrop."

Ten strides later Zeeman stood within earshot of Deidre.

"I'm sorry, Serge." She was speaking into the phone. "But, if you'd pack my clothes and grab my passport I'd be grateful." Deidre tilted her head back and laughed. "Stop wheezing, Serge. I won't be that grateful. Thank you." She rang off and turned toward Zeeman, as if she had radar. "Who's there?"

"Mike North. You are?"

"Deidre Popovitch."

"Taxi coming?" Zeeman asked, trying to confuse the reason for his proximity.

"Hopefully." She dropped her cell-phone into her purse. "But, don't hold your breath. There are only two in Hull. Once I waited for two hours."

"Public transportation needs an upgrade?"

"That's an understatement. The cabbies work when they feel like it."

Zeeman smiled at her caustic words. "Sounds like an investment opportunity."

"You're an entrepreneur?"

"I guess you could say that I dabble." Zeeman hesitated, enjoying the view her beauty provided, but not sure how to proceed. "Do you visit Hull, often?"

"More frequently than I would like." Deidre took in a sharp breath. "This is the only place where I'd feel comfortable committing suicide."

"Something I said?"

"Just having you on."

"What about car rentals?"

"There is one, but I can't direct you."

"Union rules?"

"No. I'm blind."

"Sorry."

"You're not the cause of my affliction, Mr. North."

He was silent for a moment, again unsure of himself. "What I meant was…"

"I know what you meant," she cut in, impatiently.

"Bad day?"

"Typical for me."

He considered in silence, his eyes almost closed. "I'm sorry to hear that, too."

"I don't see why. You didn't introduce me to my husband."

"Hubby's a jerk?"

"Sydney, who's around somewhere, is the ultimate jerk."

Zeeman squinted at her, amused by the blind woman's openness. "There's actually a measuring scale?"

"It's innate for women. Comes with the birth package."

"Then why, considering you built in warning mechanism, did you marry one?"

She laughed, softly. "Women also have a built-in blind spot."

"Give your husband a few minutes." The tall man shoved his hands deep in his pockets, trying to find some warmth. "I'm sure he'll come to his senses."

"Sydney has no sense. He's a panic-stricken womanizer and don't say you're sorry."

"I'm trying not to."

Deidre hesitated. "I suppose I should overlook Sydney's wanderings. But I have this foolish belief in marital fidelity."

"'Till death do you remain faithful?"

"Funny you should mention death."

"You have a morbid sense of humor?"

Deidre took a breath. "I don't suppose you're a professional killer looking for a cheap contract, payable on easy installments, with no credit check?"

Zeeman cocked an amused eyebrow, still studying her. "What have you in mind?"

"I'd like Sydney dead, or at least slightly maimed; preferably in his nether region."

"Sorry. Not my line."

Her blind eyes rolled. "I knew I'd get at least one more apology out of you."

"It slipped out."

"That's Sydney's problem in a nutshell. Every time he sees a woman, other than me, it slips out." Deidre sniffed audibly. "You smell delicious. Nothing I've experienced before. French?"

"*Ambre Topkapi.*"

"Sounds expensive."

"It was a gift."

"You could hire out smelling that good."

"I'll add that to my resume."

Deidre abruptly turned her head in the direction her husband had taken. She listened for a few seconds to the blurred sound of his voice on the breeze. Then she directed her hearing back to Zeeman.

"I'm taking a survey, Mr. North," she declared. "Are you up for it?"

"Lay it on me."

"Do you believe in life after death?"

He nodded. "There's always a chance."

"Like sex after marriage?"

"For that, I'm reliably informed, there are no guarantees." His eyes twinkled with delight as he studied all that was Deidre, from her feet to her head. "I take it you're marital discord is more physical than emotional?"

"I have both complaints, in spades."

"Long suffering?"

"Long enough to plan my husband's tour of hell."

His brow furrowed. "Starting at which level?"

"The correct term, according to Dante, is circle. Of which, there are nine. Limbo, lust, gluttony, greed, anger, heresy, violence, fraud—otherwise known as Malebolge, and treachery." Deidre raised and lowered her shoulders in a cold-fighting shiver. "I'd like to see Sydney's privates distributed in a crimson array amongst all. I don't suppose you've got fanatical religious leanings?"

"Not since I was seven."

"You'll have to forgive my vindictive personality. I get a little weirded out when it comes to Sydney."

"Otherwise you're a pussycat?"

"With a purr syndrome." She wet her lips. "Are you a man of the world, Mr. North?"

"I'd like to think so."

"In that case, how many times has someone plotted your death?"

His brows drew together darkly as he surmised that she was aware of her husband's plans. "I've irritated one or two people." He feigned ignorance with, "Are you in danger?"

"I was, until last night."

"Last night?"

"Has anyone ever killed the person who was supposed to kill you?"

"Not that I'm aware."

Deidre raised her cane a few inches, and then returned its steal tip to the walkway with a sharp click. "You cannot imagine my disappointment."

"I'd think you'd be relieved."

"When I knew the killer, I knew who to worry about." Her free hand splayed, momentarily. "Now that she's dead, I've got bupkis."

"Your killer was a woman?" Zeeman asked, continuing his ignorance ploy.

"Women make the best ones."

"Another part of the birth package?"

"Men want to believe that all females are like their mothers. As such, male defenses go down in the presence of a woman. She makes her move. He's toast. The poor bastard died not even knowing how much danger he was in."

"Some men don't have nice mothers."

Deidre gave him a crooked smile. "You're not my killer's replacement, are you?"

"I thought we'd established my lack of murderous intent."

"Ignore me. I'm in one of my moods." She forced a grin, but it quickly faded. "You didn't see a little man with a lighted foil cap get off the ferry, did you?"

Zeeman was surprised at her vague description of Steiner. "I think I would've noticed. Your husband?"

"Sydney? No. Poor Sydney has a limited skill-set. Electrifying a cap is beyond him." Deidre tapped toward Zeeman's scent, stopping when she was barely a foot away. "What about Russian gangsters?"

"Would they have been dancing the *Kalinka*?"

She jerked erect, blinking several times. "I hadn't considered that."

"Who are these gangsters, if I'm not being too nosy?"

"Their leader is Nikolay Kandinsky. Do you know him?"

Again he was surprised at her knowledge. "I know of him. Is Kandinsky chasing you?"

"I certainly hope not. I've only just qualified as a gangsterette. I'd hate to losing that standing because of my funeral."

"Are you having another mood, or should I worry about your affiliations?"

"Definitely a mood. Are you married, Mr. North?"

"Once. It didn't take."

"Mine didn't, either. But, I've still got a husband."

The tall man looked at her sideways. "You're planning on a divorce?"

"Which is entirely your fault."

"Me?"

"You wouldn't kill Sydney. You wouldn't even maim his wandering privates." Deidre gave a dramatic shrug. "That leaves divorce. Ergo, it's your fault."

"Serious, or mood?"

"Mood again."

"Well before you make another change, can you recommend a hotel?"

"My husband and I stay at his father's bed and breakfast. It's called Popovitch's. It's clean, inexpensive and on the beach. There should be plenty of room this time of the year."

"Sounds good. I'll check it out."

"You can ride with Sydney and me, assuming one of the taxis get here before we freeze to death."

"Thanks for the offer. But, I'm waiting for someone."

"Lover?"

"Business associate."

"That's no fun." Deidre turned her head abruptly in the direction of her approaching husband's footfalls. "Sydney's on his way back. Are you sure I can't offer you something to change your mind about murder? A home-cooked meal? Life-long adoration? A kitten?"

"I've got a weak spot when it comes to kittens. Let me give it some thought."

"On second thought, I'd better stick to my original plan."

"What did I miss?" he asked, guardedly.

"I'm toying with the idea of strangling my husband." Deidre raised her eyebrows high, with teasing optimism. "I don't suppose you carry a garrote? I could slip it around my husband's neck in the taxi. With Sydney's mental acuity, he wouldn't realize he was dead until we got to our cabin."

"I gave up carrying garrotes when I joined the cub scouts."

"There's never a lethal weapon around when it's needed."

"Sorry."

Deidre turned back toward his voice, grinning. "I knew I'd get another apology if I worked at it." Then her face became grim. "I can hear my husband's footsteps. Better leave."

"He's the jealous type?"

"No. But, I'm about to give him the worst day of his life. He hates to have other men see him cry."

Zeeman turned and strolled back to where Menotti waited.

"Anything?" Menotti asked.

"Lover's spat."

The taxi, a copper colored minivan, arrived.

"Who was she calling?" Menotti asked.

"Somebody named Serge." Zeeman watched as the married couple climbed into the taxi. "She wanted him to pack her clothes."

"Blind Lady's moving?"

"Divorce."

"That's fast, even for you."

"She's thinking of killing her husband."

"Seriously?"

"Blind Lady knows what he's got planned for her."

Menotti's eyes clouded with concern. "Popovitch threatened her?"

"I'm not sure. But, we'd better get to him before he gets to her. He'll have to shut her up, before she goes to the police."

The taxi drove off, leaving Zeeman wondering what could be. The brief flight of fancy ending with him remembering his history and regretting.

"I'd do anything for that woman," Zeeman murmured.

"Baby, you gotta' get it under control."

"Relax. I'm not her type."

Menotti looked taken aback. In all his years with Zeeman, there had never been a woman who had not considered the tall man her type. He let his eyes drop to the walkway, working on regaining his composure.

Menotti's bald head came up with a surprised jerk. "Wait a sec. Something just hit me."

"Tio, I can't do anything about birds."

"We never saw the Creep park the van."

"He and Leon are probably still looking for the right parking spot."

The burly man jabbed a thumb, toward the ferry. "I'm thinkin' the creep sent us on a wild goose chase."

"He's not that clever."

"Baby, you told the Creep we should search Popovitch's flat. I think that's where he went."

Zeeman's chin slowly moved up and down as he weighed his partner's words. "I'll buy that. But, I don't see that it gets us anything since Popovitch is in Hull."

Menotti's shoulders jumped, slightly. "We've got to cover the bases."

"When I suggested the search, Tio, I was assuming that Popovitch would go back home after the taxi completed its business with Blind Lady. But, Popovitch continued on with his wife. The doll's here."

"Baby, ain't nothing guaranteed."

"If Bad Man found the doll in the Popovitch's flat, he's already delivered it to Kandinsky's people."

Menotti wagged his head. "The Creep wouldn't risk handing it to anybody but Kandinsky himself. All I have to do is track the Creep down and take the doll."

"But, we don't know where Bad Man holes up."

"I've got connections."

"Your search could take days, Tio."

"Baby, I know one of Kandinsky's goons. Talkative type. He'll point me to the Creep."

"I'd better come with you."

"You can't. You've got to look out for Blind Lady."

Zeeman sighed heavily, worry showing in his handsome face. "Bad Man's more dangerous than he looks, Tio. Don't underestimate him."

"More dangerous than me?" Menotti scoffed. "Baby, he don't know what dangerous is."

"Tio…"

Zeeman felt Menotti's hand touch his arm, lightly.

"Don't sweat it, Baby. I'll be back sometime after dark."

Menotti hurried back to the ferry.

Chapter 9
Accommodations"

When the taxi arrived at Popovitch's Resort, gull screes and the scent of fish floated on the frigid wind. Zeeman paid the driver and climbed out. As the cab drove away, the tall man made a meal out of stretching his limbs. He was giving his eyes time to wander as they evaluated the surrounding risks. He saw none.

There were no people in view. But, there was a vehicle. It was an old yellow Cadillac parked in the turnaround fronting the main house. From the way the machine sagged, it was overdue for maintenance.

The building was many decades old but well kept. Its canted roof was covered by green shingles and there was the usual collection of power and phone lines running from a creosoted pole to the structure. The building's upper three floors contained evenly spaced rectangular windows, set within decorative shutters. From the repetitive drapery, it looked like one window for each guest-room. The first floor had a large expanse of glass, cloaked from within by heavy red hangings. The siding was cream in color. The wood trim was bright white. An expansive concrete porch stuck out from the foundation on the front side. Decorating it were several patio tables encircled by collections of chairs. Another door, along the building's side, provided secondary entrance and egress. Four concrete steps lead up to it.

Half a dozen cabins sat about ten yards behind the main house. These were recent additions, built upon individual concrete slabs. Each dwelling was about the size of a single car garage with a rounded roof and the same paint coloring as the main building. The cabins were designed with a single front window and separate air conditioning units. Each structure appeared to have only one way in. None of the cabins seemed to be occupied.

The main building's side door abruptly opened. An elderly man, more bones than flesh, escorted Mrs. Popovitch out and down the stairs. He wore a light blue suit, several years out of style. A chunky

young man followed, struggling under the weight of the blind
woman's suitcases. His moon face was ruddy and freckled, his hair
the color of rust. The young man's attire consisted of painter pants,
running shoes and a floral shirt.

While Zeeman studied the odd trio, the elderly man escorted
Mrs. Popovitch toward the cabin nearest the beach. The teenager
lagged behind, pausing for breath as the heavy cases banged against
his stubby legs.

At the cabin, the old man slid a key into the door lock and gave
the knob a turn. He pushed the door wide and led the blind woman
inside.

The young man rallied his efforts when he neared the cabin but
his hurried movements dumped him against the door jamb and the
large case struck his groin. He screamed in agony and collapsed to
his knees.

The elderly man's hand reappeared just long enough to grab the
offending suitcase and take it inside. The young man clawed up the
jamb to his feet. Then he hobbled into the cabin.

Several minutes passed. Then the two males came out. The
elderly man pulled the door shut. He headed back toward the main
house. The young man minced after, moving knock-kneed, one hand
gripping his crotch, grim pain showing in his pale cheeks.

Zeeman straightened his tie. Then, he strode to the main building
and went inside through the front door.

The drapes blocked out the sun. The room's only source of
illumination was half a dozen lighted candles. Various electronic
light fixtures on furniture and walls were unused. The parquet floor
held a sprinkling of armless seating, presumably to lend a homey
atmosphere. A small, ornate desk with a Japanned finish rested near
the room's center. Upon this furnishing sat an opened guest-
registration book, and a brass lamp; also unlit. Behind the desk was
a secretary style chair. The room's remaining furniture consisted of
several round tables and a large bookcase filled with paperbacks.
The walls were papered in purple-striped beige. This vertical space
was decorated with uniformly spread abstract reproductions.

To Zeeman's left, blue and orange flames lapped at the
protective glass front of a gas-fueled stone fireplace. The blaze gave
off welcome heat and a modicum of footlight. To his right, a

staircase led to the upper floors and the door through which the trio had exited.

Zeeman stopped at mid-room and listened while his eyes continued to drift. The shadowy interior was not unlike that of a small museum, but filled with imitations. There was light enough to view the displays. But not enough to reveal each items deception. Even the smell was museum-like: moldy dust from decaying artifacts. There was absolute silence.

Then the side door creaked opened.

A moment later, the old man staggered in. His feet flapped on the parquet like duck-webs on plate-glass. Each breath came in with a gasp and left with an asthmatic wheeze. His face was gaunt. He was all hollow eyes and jutting nose. The plastic nametag on his suit read 'Jerome Popovitch.'

The young man trailed in. He pulled the door closed. His ruddy mug, in its natural state, offered a confused expression. His nametag read 'Charlie Owens.' He had small, evil eyes: the type that never stopped moving. At the moment, they were gauging Zeeman

"Can I help you, sir?" the elder Popovitch asked, when he caught sight of Zeeman.

Zeeman nodded. "Room."

He walked to the desk, his movements unhurried, his eyes more concerned with the dim-looking youth's constant stare.

"How long will you be with us, Mr…"

"Mike North," Zeeman returned. "One, maybe two days."

Jerome completed his duck walk to the swivel, and sat down. There, he repeated the name Zeeman had offered thoughtfully, as if the moniker meant something.

"You look familiar, Mr. North," Owens remarked, as he sauntered over to the desk.

"I've got that kind of face," Zeeman returned.

"Here for the fishing?"

"Business." Zeeman refocused his attention on the old man. "There's an outside chance that I'll need to stay longer. Will that be a problem?"

Jerome wagged his head. "I have a nice room on the second floor overlooking the beach."

"I'd prefer something on top, overlooking the approach road."

"What d'you want to see the road for?" Owens asked, his suspicion evident.

"Taxi. I'll be calling one in the morning. That okay with you?"

"Oh, yes, of course," Jerome cut in.

The elderly man opened a desk drawer and rummaged through a pile of keys. He selected one and handed it to Zeeman.

"This should fit your needs, Mr. North."

The young man grinned, showing a span of greenish teeth. "For a second, I thought you were running from the cops."

"Stop thinking," Zeeman warned.

The youth's grin faded.

Jerome said, "I don't see luggage, Mr. North."

"Screw-up at the airport." Zeeman made a vague movement with one hand. "I couldn't help but notice the candles."

"Power outage."

"Transformer shorted," Owens enjoined. "Electric company's been notified."

"They'll repair it tonight?" Zeeman asked.

"Probably not," Jerome said. "Maybe tomorrow." His sunken chest heaved as he drew in a labored breath. "There are other hotels. Closer to town. They haven't been affected by the outage. I can arrange a reservation."

"I like candles."

Jerome pushed the registration book toward the front of the desk. "Will you sign, please?"

"Common problem, power outages?" Zeeman scrawled the name, *'Mike North'*, listing his city of residence as Phoenix.

"Five, maybe six a year," Owens said.

"Common enough."

"More than we would like," said the elderly man, agreeably.

Charlie Owens snorted. "Hull ain't Boston. So it sucks hind tit when it comes to good equipment."

"That's Charlie's opinion," Jerome quickly put in.

"Everybody says the same thing, Pop," the young man protested.

"What Charlie's telling you is that some folks in Hull don't care for politicians and their inaction."

Zeeman said, "Most folks, everywhere, don't like politicians."

The young man grinned again.

Jerome turned the ledger around and looked at the tall man's signature. "Welcome to Popovitch's Bed and Breakfast, Mr. North." His sunken eyes moved to the fireplace. "You're probably wondering about heat. No electricity means no forced air heating."

"A chill crossed my mind."

"Each room has its own gas fireplace," Owens interrupted. "Gas water heaters. Plenty of heat and hot water."

"Sounds good."

"How would you like to pay, Mr. North?" the elder Popovitch asked.

"Cash." Zeeman took out the remains of his money. He peeled off five twenties and set them on the desk. "Enough for tonight?"

Jerome opened the desk's center drawer and pulled out a flat, steel box. He lifted the top, dropped in the money. Then he took out several smaller bills. These he handed back.

"I'll need to see your identification, Mr. North," the old man said. "It's the law."

"The cops got nothing better to do than worry about travelers," complained Owens. "Man, like if they're real cops, they'd go after the real criminals."

Zeeman took out his wallet. He removed an Arizona driving license. The plastic card was embossed with a dark-haired man's photo, a close match to Zeeman, but not him. The name on the license was, 'Michael North.' He handed it to the elderly Popovitch.

"Thank you, Mr. North," the old man politely returned.

"Hot this time of year in Arizona?" Owens asked, still curious about Zeeman.

"Hotter than here." Zeeman addressed the old man with: "What do I do for light, in case I want to read?"

Jerome opened one of the desk's side drawers. From within he took out a handful of long narrow candles. He set them on the desktop.

"You have matches, Mr. North?" Owens asked.

"Lighter." Zeeman picked up the candles.

"I have a kerosene lantern, if you'd prefer," Jerome offered.

"Candles are good." Zeeman pocketed the wax sticks and the cash. "What time do you lock and unlock the outside doors?"

"Midnight and six. But, if you plan to be…"

"That works." The tall man looked around, again, taking note of Charlie Owens's continued curious stare. "Other guests?"

"Off season," Owens replied. "Other than Pop, you'll be the only one in the main house."

"Inn keeping must be a tough way to meet ends."

"You should've come last week. Tourists everywhere."

"We've been booked solid all year, until this week," the old man put in. "Surprisingly good."

Charlie Owens cut in with, "Shriners. Teachers. Senior Citizens. We even had a bunch of nuns." He swallowed, his Adams apple bobbing twice. "It's been one pain-in-the-ass group after another, all year."

The front entrance opened and closed. All three men turned toward the noise of approaching footsteps.

Seconds later, a stubby man who looked like a cross between a beetle and a peccary waddled in, all jaws and bowed legs. He was in a sheriff's uniform, including a Trooper's hat. The metal nametag on his chest, above the badge, read: 'D. Sherman'

"Got a minute, Jerome?" Sherman asked, his eyes on Zeeman.

Charlie Owens looked startled and quickly retreated from the desk, into the shadows.

"What's up, Don?" the elder Popovitch asked.

The Sheriff went over and purposely gave Zeeman a dismissing glare. "There's a private matter to discuss."

Zeeman's face showed a momentary concern. After it passed, Zeeman made a vague mention of taking a walk. Then he went out the way he had come in. But instead of leaving the porch tall man lingered near the door, and listened.

"What's wrong?" Jerome asked.

"It's about Sydney," the sheriff returned.

"The taxi dropped him at Hasty Car Rental on his way here. He wanted something to drive during him and Deidre's stay."

"I know. That's where I arrested him," Sherman announced.

Jerome bleated, "What in hell's my son done now?"

"Boston Police want Sydney held for questioning."

"Sid didn't do nothing, Pop. Just another cop hassle."

"Sydney's a person of interest in the murder of Meri Darling," the Sheriff explained. "Boston P-D's on the way to Hull. They'll talk to Sydney here. If there's anything to their evidence, Sydney will be taken back for charges."

"Murder?" the old man croaked, with horror.

"No way, man," the teen declared. "Sid maybe screwed up a couple times, but he's no killer."

"I'm sorry, Jerome," the Sheriff said. "But, I talked to the chief investigator. There's good reason for their suspicions."

"Like what, man? Not buying 'em coffee and donuts?"

"You're not helping, Charlie," Sherman warned.

"What were you told?" the elder Popovitch asked.

"Sydney was involved with the dead woman, professionally and personally."

"Don, my son's happily married."

"There's more. The night Meri Darling died, he was with her. I asked your son about it. He admitted meeting with the dead woman at his flat. He denied killing her. But he's as nervous as a cat in a room full of wooden rockers, which is a good indication of guilt."

"I just don't believe it."

"According to the information given Boston P.D., your son had been participating in some kind of smuggling along with Meri Darling. If I were to hazard a guess, it was drugs and Sydney killed her in some coked up frenzy."

"Don't listen, Pop. Sid might do a line or two when he gets tensed, but he ain't no doper."

"You've known Sydney all his life, Don. Do you really see him as a killer?"

"It's not for me to say, Jerome," Sherman said. "I hope, for once, you're right about Sydney."

"Who told you that my son was involved with that woman?"

"Boston P.D. received a call. That's all I know."

Charlie Owens piped up with, "Sid was in love with Meri. That's how I know he'd never kill her. And she was in love with him. They were gonna' get married."

"How'd you come by that?" Sherman demanded.

There was a pause. Then Owens said, "Sid and Meri told me. I met 'em in Boston a couple weeks ago."

"How was he going to get married when he was already married?"

"I dunno."

For nearly a minute Zeeman stood and stared at the door, embarrassed by realization. Meri had conned him yet again. Her vindictiveness and greed, he understood. He had experienced years of it. But, she should have been straight within about the Bling-blings. About her plans to marry Popovitch.

The Sheriff's voice hardened. "Charlie, why in hell didn't you come forward with what you knew about Sydney when the murder broke on the news?"

"Sid's a friend, man. A guy doesn't piss on his friends."

"Well, how about helping law enforcement for a change, and tell me the rest of what Sid told you, before I haul your ass in on charges of obstructing justice."

"You can't do that, man."

"I can and I will. And after I've got your drug dealing ass in jail, I'll send my men over to search your apartment. They'll have instructions to tear the place apart. How much cocaine do you think they'll find, Charlie?"

"Look, man," returned Owens. "All I know is that when a guy's wife hands a guy shit, he looks around for somebody else. But he sure as shit don't kill who he finds. If Sid was going to kill anybody, it'd been Deidre."

"Don, my son loves his wife," the elderly man protested.

"They ain't been in love for years, Pop. Sorry, man. But, that's the way it is."

"You don't like Deidre, Charlie?" Sherman asked.

"I got nothing against her, man. But, Sid says she can be a real pain in the ass."

There was silence.

Eventually Sheriff Sherman said, "Jerome, did Deidre tell you anything about Meri Darling's murder?"

"No," the old man replied.

"Did she ever mentioned Meri Darling?"

"Hey, man, this is police brutality," Charlie Owens intervened. "You need a lawyer, Pop. Don't say another word."

"I'd never heard of Meri Darling until I read about her murder," the elderly Popovitch said.

"Jerome, does the name Harry Steiner mean anything to you?" Sherman asked.

"I don't recall it."

"I heard about Steiner," chimed Owens. "Guy's crazy. A killer. A regular bloodletting freak show. He killed his whole family."

How does this Steiner fit with my son?"

"Harry Steiner broke out of Bridgewater State Hospital five or six years ago," Sheriff Sherman said.

"Why was he in there?"

"Like Charlie said. He killed his whole family."

"He's been loose all this time?"

"He's constantly moving around. That makes him very hard to find."

"He raped and murdered one of the hospital nurses, man."

"And my son was working for this man?"

"That's what I was told," the sheriff replied.

"Steiner's nobody to mess with, man. Sid wanted to stop smuggling. But Steiner wouldn't let him out of it."

"Steiner," said Sherman, "is alleged to have connections with a Russian mobster named Nikolay Kandinsky. Does Kandinsky's name ring any bells with either of you?"

"Not to me." The old man's voice sounded bewildered.

"Everybody's heard of Kandinsky, man." There was the sound of pride in the young man's voice.

"Did Sydney talk to you about Nikolay Kandinsky, Charlie?" Sherman pressed.

A moment of foot-shuffling silence passed before the teenager said, "Word gets around, man."

"Don, maybe this Steiner person killed that woman?" the old man suggested.

"That's what Sydney said. But we both know how Sydney blames others whenever he gets into trouble."

"If Sid said Steiner did her, man, then Steiner did her."

"It's possible," returned Sherman. "But, the evidence says otherwise." The sheriff paused a beat. "The investigation's ongoing, Jerome. There are other suspects. Nobody's trying to railroad Sydney. I'll keep you informed, as best I can, of what Boston P.D. tells me."

The old man's voice became hesitant. "My son's a computer programmer. How could he get involved with such people?"

"Sydney hasn't done computer work for years."

"Gambling again?"

"One of my questions to Sydney," said Sherman. "He denied it. But, that would explain why he would be desperate enough to form these alliances." There was another pause. "Look, Jerome, even if Sydney's right about Steiner killing Meri Darling, that still leaves a problem."

"What problem?"

"Apparently, Sydney conspired with Meri Darling to kill Deidre."

"That's ridiculous."

"Boston P.D. has tape recordings that prove otherwise."

"Deidre didn't say a thing to me."

"One last thing, Jerome," Sherman said. "Boston P.D. issued a BOLO for Tio Menotti and Mike Zeeman after being unable to locate the pair at the address they gave their parole officers. I don't expect Menotti or Zeeman to come to Hull. But if anybody with those names shows up here, call me."

"Yes, of course," the old man sighed.

There was a short span of silence.

Sherman said, "Jerome, I'd like you to encourage Sydney to cooperate with us. It's in his best interests to tell us what he knows."

"Don't do it, Pop. It's a trap, man."

"One last thing, Jerome. I'll need to speak with Deidre as soon as possible."

"I'll take you to her," Jerome said.

"It's better if I speak to her formally. You know, at the station."

"Deidre won't know anything, man," Owens insisted.

"She's blind, Charlie, not cut off from communications."

"Deidre and Sid never talk," the youth insisted. "All they do is fight."

"I'll drive Deidre to the police station," the old man interrupted.

"Thank you," Sherman said.

There was another short stretch of silence.

"Who was the big guy just here?" the Sheriff asked.

"Mr. North," Jerome replied. "Why?"

"Did he have a reservation?"

"No. Mr. North is here on business."

"What kind of business?"

"He didn't say."

"Did North pay by credit card?"

"No. Cash."

"You checked his identification?"

"Of course. Arizona driving license. Phoenix address."

"All right. Just being careful." There was another pause. "I'm real sorry about this, Jerome."

The old man said, "Thanks for making the trip to tell me."

"To be honest, I wouldn't have. But with the power out I didn't think the phones would ring."

Zeeman quickly left the porch and made his way around the main building. Then he headed directly for the beach. When he reached the water's edge, the tall man looked back. The police cruiser was on its way to town. The old man was hobbling toward the cabin Deidre Popovitch occupied. He occupied himself tossing stones into the gray water as he waited.

Several minutes later Jerome, Owens and Deidre climbed into the old Cadillac and headed for Hull.

Zeeman went directly to Deidre's cabin. The cheap lock on the door delayed the tall man only a few seconds. Then he was inside.

Instinctively, Zeeman felt around in the blackness for a wall switch, and flipped it on. Nothing happened. Remembering the power outage, Zeeman took a cigarette lighter from his pocket and flicked it to life. Then, he took out a candle, put flame to the wick, and pocketed the lighter.

In the candle's yellowish glow, the tall man eyed the living space.

The room had a low, plaster ceiling with walls covered in wood panels. On the tile floor, near the center of the living space, was a yellow rug. Two lamps with jade colored plastic shades topped a small desk next to the wall, on his right. A small window, the brown drapes pulled open, occupied space above the desk. At the far end of the rug was a platform rocker. To Zeeman's left was a loveseat upholstered in a floral design. Built into the wall nearest the rocker was a stone fireplace, the ashes from a wood fire still glowing within. On a dais at the rear of the room a farm-style table was surrounded by four high-back chairs. On the same raised flooring, adjacent to the table, was a small kitchenette. The place smelled of wood smoke and a woman's perfume: Sandalwood.

For the next hour Zeeman searched the cabin. He made a point of leaving everything as he had found it. But, by the time the tall man was done he was no closer to locating the doll, and its load of Bling-blings, than before. If Popovitch had brought the doll, he had not sent it with his wife to the bed and breakfast. Since Popovitch was incarcerated and soon to be taken back to Boston, there was only one option to locate the doll. Zeeman would have to get its location from Blind Lady. He left the cabin, making certain the door locked on his way out.

Chapter 10
"A Change of Focus"

It was nearly 10:00 that night when headlights shined through the window in Mike Zeeman's room. He got off the bed, went over and looked out. The old Cadillac was back in its parking spot.

Moments later the vehicle's headlights went dark. As the tall man watched, Jerome climbed out into cold moonlight and hobbled around to the rider's side. He opened the door, his breath laboring out in plumes of white. Then, the elderly man reached into the vehicle and assisted Deidre in leaving it. As they headed for her cabin, Zeeman slipped on his overcoat and left. He was in no great hurry. He would speak with Deidre. But, not until her father-in-law had left her alone.

Outside, the cold air slapped Zeeman's face. He turned up his coat collar and casually headed around the main house to the beach side. With each step, his shoes crunched on the frosty brown grass. When Deidre's cabin came into view, Zeeman spotted the elderly man. Jerome was on his way to the main house, alone.

Zeeman waited until the old fellow was inside. Then he trotted over to the cabin.

After glancing around to make sure that he was not being observed, Zeeman put an ear to the door. Beyond, he heard soft footfalls. These were followed by the slow, rhythmic rattle of water cascading through a pipe. The tall man stood erect and took a deep breath before rapping his knuckles on the wood.

"It's open, Pop," Deidre called, from the other side.

Zeeman turned the knob and followed the door inward.

Kindling had been added to the fireplace since his search. What had been ashes and coals was brightly burning flames. The lapping blaze filled the cabin with golden light and cozy warmth. His eyes drifted. Deidre was in the kitchenette. She stood at the sink filling a teakettle with water, her back to Zeeman. A white cane rested against her hip. She wore a thin, dark, dress with a sailor collar. The slash-pocket skirt flared slightly just above her knees. Her calves were bare. She wore fuzzy slippers on her feet. The firelight, hitting the blind woman's clinging ensemble, outlined a nice complement of curves. The tall man shut the door, admiring all that was her.

"I'm sorry, Pop," Deidre declared, over one shoulder. "But, nothing you say will change my mind. Sydney planned to kill me. The recordings prove it. It's up to the police, now."

Deidre turned off the water, and grabbed her cane. Then looping the stick's handle-strap over one wrist, she made her way to the stove. The blind woman set the teakettle on a burner and turned on the heating element.

"It's not Pop," Zeeman declared.

Deidre whirled toward the sound of his voice. "Who are you?" The words trembled past her lips. "What do you want?"

"It's Mike North."

"North?" she echoed, thinking. As if in silent prayer, her free hand went to a silver broach, in the shape of a cross, pinned above her right breast. "Mr. North. Yes, I remember. You're the apology-man from the Taxi-stand." The blind woman smiled faintly.

"Sorry I frightened you."

"Late at night, a man comes to my cabin, and what does he do?" she said. "He offers an apology." Deidre extended one hand toward the counter next to the stove, sidled over and leaned back against it. "What does that say about me, Mr. North?" She leaned the cane within reach. "Am I such a pitiful creature?"

Between the blind woman's slightly parted lips Zeeman saw the glint of white teeth. He liked the shape of her mouth. The lips were full, offering the promise of pleasure. He dipped his eyes to the long fingers on her slender hands. The nails were unpainted, but manicured. He wondered how she could maintain them so perfectly without being able to see.

Zeeman smiled. "If you were single I'd be camped on your doorstep."

"You're making me blush."

"It looks good on you."

"Now, you're beginning to worry me."

The tall man hesitated. "I took your advice and got a room here."

"Then, it's my turn to apologize."

"How so?"

"I had no idea the power was off when I suggested Pop's place."

"Minor inconvenience."

Deidre frowned in the direction of Zeeman's voice. "Slumming? Or, lost?"

"Neither. I came to explain."

"Dear God please do not let this man offer another apology."

Zeeman took several steps away from the door. and scanned the cabin, his eyes searching for anything new. Not seeing changes, the tall man returned his stare to her.

"I sort of misled you," he said.

"Don't worry. I'm used to it."

He gave her a confused look. "But, I've only done it this one time."

"I meant being misled in general."

"Ah. This happens often?"

"Ask anyone who's blind. We're always preyed upon. In my case, the perpetrator is usually my husband. Unlike you, Sydney always denies his deceptions, even when his guilt is irrefutable. I guess you could say that my husband is the poster boy for incompetence."

"That's not good news for me."

"Imagine how I feel. I married the man." She licked her lips. "Tell me something. How does one 'sort of mislead'?"

He squinted at her with confusion. "Come again?"

"You said you sort of misled me. In my experience, one either misleads or one doesn't."

"Ah. In that case, I misled."

"That must put you in the Guinness Book of Records."

"I think that one missed me, too."

"You and I have a ten minute relationship, based entirely upon apologies and your wonderful cologne, and you've already led me on. That must be some sort of record."

"In my own defense, I did so without malice."

"Dare I ask what might be forthcoming? Empty promises of devotion? Or worse, unconjugated verbs?"

"Sorry."

"A little help, here, God? This man is going to apologize me to death." The blind woman crossed her arms, grinning at nothing. "Now that we've gotten what I hope will be your last apology out of the way, how did you mislead me?"

Zeeman moved across the front room, into the kitchenette. "My real reason for coming to Hull was to meet your husband."

"Sydney?" she said, her voice rising in surprise. "You poor man. No one should be that lonely."

"Is he here?" He feigned ignorance of the afternoon's events.

"Lucky you. Sydney's been arrested. What did you want to see him about?"

"Your husband contacted me about a business opportunity." He shrugged his broad shoulders. "I'm curious. Why was your husband arrested?"

"Murder. Conspiracy to commit murder. A litany of other felonies." She smiled briefly. "My husband's a man of non-sterling qualities."

"Are you in another of your moods?"

"No. That's the truth."

"Who'd your husband kill?"

"Meri Darling." Deidre's eyebrows formed a dark, thoughtful 'V'. "She and Sydney were having an affair." Her breath sucked in, sharply. "God, I hope Sydney didn't murder every woman he screwed. The police will have to establish a new definition for serial killers."

"Surly there's more than infidelity to support your husband's guilt?"

"Mr. North, you sound like a bleeding heart liberal." There was a touch of humor in her voice. "One of those close-minded types who requires a signed confession before acknowledging the premise of guilt."

"I'm merely of the opinion that extramarital wanderings don't necessarily create a killer."

Her arms rose and fell. "Leave it to me to bring the good old boy network to Sydney's defense." Deidre's hands went to the counter, accidentally rattling the cane. "Frankly, Mr. North, I'm disappointed."

"Would you like another apology or a plea for sympathy?"

"No apologies. I don't want to lose the buzz I'm getting from your cologne."

"I'm curious. How long have you and your husband been married?"

"You're wondering why I'm not Sydney's devoted slave?"

"Something like that."

"My husband and I entered our wedded nightmare two plus years ago—a lifetime of agony, or so it seems."

"I'm…"

"Don't even think about apologizing."

"How did you meet?"

"Oddly enough, we first met when Sydney saved me from being murdered." A crooked grin spread one side of her beautiful face. "At the time he was my hero." Abruptly somberness returned to her. "Little did I know the truth about my Sydney."

"Meaning his affair with Meri Darling?"

"Her and others."

Zeeman walked to the kitchen table and sat down. "I find it odd that your husband saved your life only to plot your death."

"To tell the truth, I wasn't really in any danger the day we met." She reached out and took the cane in hand. "It was right after I'd lost my sight. I was tapping my way across an intersection. The light changed. Only, I didn't know it." Her face, momentarily, closed in thought. "Blind people don't notice light changes. The units make a warning beep, of course. When you're in the middle of the road and can't hear anything but engines noises, the beeping doesn't register.

"One of the drivers waiting for me to cross called for volunteers in a lynching. Another shouted something about having a rope." Deidre gave her head a determined nod, blindly facing Zeeman's voice. "That's when another voice chimed that a light pole would serve to string me up." She twisted her mouth into a purse, remembering. "At that point, somebody grabbed my arm."

He frowned. "You were actually attacked in a road crossing?"

"At the time, I thought it was the lynch mob. So I struck out with my cane." The blind woman shifted her weight from one leg to the other. "But, it was Sydney. He said, 'Lady, if I don't' get you across in the next twenty seconds we're both dead.'" Deidre dipped her chin, scraping the cane lazily back and forth. "I guess we made it. We're still alive."

"You sound disappointed."

"Of course I'm disappointed. I actually married Sydney 'The Philanderer' Popovitch."

"You knew he wasn't the faithful type?"

"I suspected from the beginning," she returned. "Any woman who marries a handsome man has to. But, one lives in hope that one's husband is the exception. Hope, of course, died when I discovered that Meri Darling and Sydney were going to kill me. You cannot imagine my embarrassment. How could I have been so gullible?"

"Your husband was going to marry her?"

Her head wagged. "Their plan was to kill me for my life insurance." She let go a long sigh. "I suppose if you're going to be killed by the person you love, life insurance is as good a reason as any. Nevertheless, it seems so commercial. Kill your wife and have a happy holiday. Kill your wife and travel the world."

The floor vibrated as a log collapsed in the fireplace. This was followed by a loud snap and crackle. A flare of light flashed throughout the cabin. The blaze chased shadows over furnishings, up walls and across the ceiling like racing cats.

"Insurance killings are tricky," Zeeman observed. "They take planning."

She cocked her head. "Have you been a naughty boy?"

"Murder for insurance isn't part of my history."

The steam whistled from the kettle. Deidre grabbed the handle with her free hand, carried the vessel to the dining table, and set it down.

"Tea?" she offered.

"It'll keep me up."

"I've been serving Sydney the wrong drinks."

Deidre collected a teabag from a tin on the counter and a cup and saucer from a cupboard. She brought these to the table and sat down across from Zeeman.

He reached over and placed the teabag in the cup and then poured in water from the teakettle.

"What if I told you that your husband had nothing to do with Meri's murder?" He returned the kettle to the table.

"'Meri's murder'? That's very telling, Mr. North."

"I don't understand."

"You find her death a personal loss." She thrust a finger toward his voice. "You were involved with Meri Darling."

His chin dipped, a smile of incredulity forming.

"Your silence tells me that you're 'sort of' misleading me, again."

"I was married to her for a short time," the tall man admitted.

"The marriage that didn't take?"

"Meri was a great toy. But she made a lousy wife."

"Meri was interested only in Meri?"

"Yes," he said. "That fits her. How did you discover their plans to kill you?"

"I recorded their phone conversations," she returned. "I've done so for the past month. My friend, Serge Vasiliev, set everything up. He's very clever." Her tongue darted out of her mouth, and wetted her lips several times. "How do you earn your living, Mr. North?"

"I'm a jeweler," he lied.

"A jeweler who came to Hull to see Sydney, who used to be married to Meri Darling. Will miracles never cease?"

He noisily cleared his throat. "You said you'd met Sydney after losing your sight. Were you injured in an accident?"

"Glaucoma."

"You don't look old enough."

"It's usually a disease of older people. But, Glaucoma can hit any time after adulthood." Her eyebrows came together. "In my case, I didn't realize what was happening until it was too late."

"There's nothing doctors can do?"

"I'm told they'll be able to transplant entire eyeballs, in the future." Deidre gave the world a crooked grin. "The trick, from my end, is to live long enough."

Zeeman fell silent, doing a stint of serious thinking. He had made a mistake, telling her about his marriage. He wasn't sure how it had been the wrong move. But, he sensed that she knew who he really was.

"You're not speaking, Mr. North," she said, after a while. "When Sydney doesn't speak it means I've caught him in a lie."

Zeeman shifted in the chair. "I was just wondering how I was going to complete my business, with your husband being inaccessible."

"You're here about the Bling-blings, aren't you?"

He was surprised that she knew what was in the doll. But, Zeeman managed to keep his cool.

"Do you have them?" he asked.

"No. Only Sydney knows where they are."

"Can you get a message to him?"

"As you can imagine, considering that I had Sydney arrested, he and I are not talking."

"Would your husband have given the diamonds to someone he trusted?"

"As far as I know, they're still in the doll used to smuggle the stones from France. If he gave the doll to somebody, he didn't say."

"Did your husband bring the doll here?"

"It's not like I could watch him pack. But, he wouldn't have left it at home."

"How can you be sure?"

"Not even Sydney's that stupid." The blind woman spread her hands. "But as to what he did with the doll after it arrived here, I don't have a clue."

"What about his father?"

"Not a chance. Pop's getting senile. He'd hide the doll and forget where he put it."

"What about Charlie Owens?"

"Hand Charlie anything worth money and he'd sell it." She wet her lips. "How much of the diamonds are you interested in?"

"All of them."

"Sydney says they're worth a million."

He rubbed the knuckles of one hand along his jaw. "Try half that."

"Half a million's a big difference of opinion."

"I'm in business to make a profit, Mrs. Popovitch."

Deidre bit her lip thoughtfully. "When are you going to leave Hull?"

"In the morning. Why?"

"I'm pretty sure the police will let me speak to Sydney. There's nothing they like better than to record a telephone conversation between a suspect and the suspect's wife." She shrugged. "Let's say Sydney tells me where to find the doll. We're talking cash?"

"If we can come to terms."

"Stop by around 10:00, tomorrow morning."

Zeeman got to his feet. "Okay. I'll be back."

"Before you leave, may I touch your face?"

"Why?"

"To know what you look like. Do you mind?"

His uneasiness went into overdrive. But there was no way around it if he was to keep her confidence. He would have to comply with her request.

"Help yourself."

The blind woman stood, grabbed her cane and tapped around the table in the direction of his voice.

Zeeman quickly closed the gap. He gripped Deidre by her waist, instinctively drawing her close.

She hung the crook of the cane around her neck and reached up with both hands. Then, for nearly a minute, her fingers lightly followed the contours of his face. When the blind woman finished, her eyebrows went up, and her lips formed a surprised 'O'. There was a flush to her cheeks.

"Too much cologne?" he asked.

"You're very handsome."

Deidre stepped out of his grasp.

"Your fingers probably need retreading."

Her head wagged. "No chance."

Zeeman turned and made his way to the cabin door. Looking over at her, sudden pity showed in his face. His eyes dipped away from her blind stare. Unexpected compassion surged through him. He wanted to end this gig. But leaving would do no good. With Popovitch in jail it would not be long before Kandinsky or Steiner would confront Blind Lady.

Zeeman opened the door. As he left, he gave Deidre another look. She was helpless. It was easy to imagine what the Russian and Bad Man would do to her.

Chapter 11
"Unexpected Return"

Outside Deidre's cabin, the night air gave Zeeman the shivers. Black clouds overhead blocked the stars and moon. A cold wind carried the promise of more snow. His breath was a white, smoke-like vapor. From the beach came the surf's steady rush, and retreat.

A door creaked open. Zeeman twisted toward the sound.

Menotti came out of the main house's side exit. The burly man stopped on the frosty grass and looked around, as if not sure what to do.

"Tio," Zeeman called.

"My balls are freezin'," Menotti returned. He hurried over to his partner, puffing like a workhorse pulling a plow. "I hope you got good news, Baby."

"The doll's here." The tall man's eyebrows went up. "But, Blind Lady says she doesn't know where it's hidden."

"I saw Popovitch and a bunch of Boston's finest at the ferry as I got off."

"Popovitch has been arrested for Meri's murder."

"I guess that settles who did her in."

"Since when do the cops get anything right?"

Menotti inclined his head slightly. "You believe her about the doll?"

"Not completely. She knows about the Bling-blings."

"Baby, that ain't good."

"She's interested in selling the stones. She's going to call her husband to find out where the doll is."

"That sounds positive."

"Unfortunately, as part of my cover I told her that Popovitch had approached me to sell the Bling-blings."

Menotti raised his brows and stared at his partner. "He'll blow that as soon as she mentions it. So, what do we do?"

"I left it with her to come back in the morning."

"You think she'll make a run for it?"

"If she does, she'll take the doll along."

"And risk having you show up to take it?"

"Popovitch will probably assume that we work for Bad Man. Whether he does or not, he won't want the doll left here." The cold wind brought the sound of the ferry's diesels as the vessel chugged its way toward Boston. "I think he'll tell her where it is. I think he'll tell her to deliver it directly to Kandinsky."

"That's a lot to expect. The poor woman's blind."

"From what she said about her husband, he's never given too much thought to her."

"Any chance we can get her to sell the Bling-blings out from under hubby?"

"I think so. I offered her half a million."

Menotti's round face showed bewilderment. "Where in hell are we going to get half a million?"

"We'll sell the stones and split the proceeds. Just like we planned with Meri."

"Meaning Blind Lady gets half?"

"She has the diamonds. We don't."

The burly man put his hands in his pockets and looked away. "I guess it doesn't matter."

Zeeman rubbed his forehead, pushing his dark hair back. "You found Bad Man?"

"I found his flop. He wasn't there. His landlord said he ain't been around in three days." Menotti tilted toward Zeeman, slightly. "The Creep's been busy since we saw him."

"What did he do?"

"I found an old man lying on the floor in Popovitch's flat." Menotti wiped his eyes, with the back of each hand. "Shot by something with a small caliber."

"Dead?"

"He was alive when I left him. But from the blood loss, I wouldn't take any bets on survival."

Zeeman gave his partner a worried look. "You got the guy some help, right?"

"I called emergency services. But with that BOLO out on us, I couldn't hang around."

"Who was the old man?"

"I checked his wallet. Name's Vasiliev.

Zeeman gazed around, muttering under his breath, remembering Deidre's telephone conversation.

"Baby, what's wrong?"

"Blind Lady asked him to get her clothes and passport. You're sure Bad Man shot him?"

"No. But, whoever did it was probably doing a search when the old man arrived. Who else but the Creep would break and toss a dump like that?"

"I buy your search theory. But, how did you come by Vasiliev getting shot while it was happening?"

"The old fellow was sprawled on top of a bunch of books that had been dumped from the bookcase."

Zeeman's shoulders lifted slightly. "Is Kandinsky still out of town?"

"You can forget about Kandinsky."

"What do you mean?"

"Dead."

Zeeman was momentarily at a loss. "What happened?"

"Somebody put two rounds into the top of the Russian's head while he was taking a piss in one of the airport's toilets." Menotti's eyes darted across his surroundings. "The cops figure the shooter was in the ventilation duct."

"Sounds like a small shooter."

"According to my contact in the Russian mob, those air-return ducts are big enough to hold the Creep."

"That's who they suspect?"

"Top of their list."

"Where was Kandinsky's bodyguard?"

"The Russian had trouble letting go in front of strangers—if you get my drift." Menotti made a vague movement with one hand. "He always left his guard at the entrance to redirect anybody who came in need. That left Kandinsky in private with his hand on the throttle, not realizing that somebody was taking aim from above." He made a long pull on the cigar and blew a stream of smoke toward the black sky. "At least he died feeling relieved."

"The guard must've heard the shot."

"He says not."

"But..."

"When Kandinsky seemed to be taking longer, than usual, the guard went to check. Found his boss dead." Menotti made a casual shrug. "No witnesses. Shooter made a clean getaway. Small caliber gun."

"As much as I like Bad Man for the hit, how did he know that Kandinsky would make a pit stop? He'd have to have been waiting in the vents, so how would he know which facility the Kandinsky would use? See what I mean?"

"Kandinsky's got prostate problems." Menotti smiled but his voice remained flat. "It's common knowledge. That guy never passed up a chance to pee. Speaking of which, I could use a little relief myself."

"So all Bad Man had to do was find out Kandinsky's flight number, and crawl through the ductwork to the facility closest to where the plane docked."

"There'd be no guarantees. But if I was Kandinsky I'd take a piss there after a long flight."

Zeeman shoved his hands into his coat pockets. "What's the Russian mob going to do now that they've penciled Bad Man in for Kandinsky's death?"

"They've put an open contract out on him—half a million, no questions asked. I told my contact with the Russians that we'd want in."

"Sounds tasty. But, I don't see us finding him."

"My money says the Creep's on his way here." The burly man lit a cigar; noisily sucking on the end as clouds of acrid smoke belched out. "We get the diamonds from Blind Lady. We do the hit on the Creep. I call that a nice evening's work."

Silence fell between the two. Menotti puffed his cigar and stamped his feet, trying to warm his toes. Zeeman looked around, offering up more mutterings.

"What if Blind Lady comes up empty?" Menotti man asked.

"Then we whack Bad Man, collect and head to California."

"That works." Menotti raised his left arm and pulled back his coat to get a look at his watch. "Maybe she's got the doll in her cabin?"

"I searched."

"Maybe she's got a hidey-hole?"

"I went through the place, top to bottom, Tio. Nothing."

A garbage barge, making its way out to sea, chugged past, fifty yards from the beach. Gulls followed, flying above looking for a chance to land. The barge's lights winked on the wave tops. Behind the vessel its wake surged, generating foam and rolling currents.

"Baby, I been doing another rethink."

Zeeman rolled his eyes. "You're always doing a rethink."

"What if Blind Lady's in cahoots with the Creep?"

"Tio, no woman in her right mind gets involved with Bad Man."

"Meri did."

"Meri's dead. And her arrangement with Bad Man had nothing to do with choice."

"Okay. What about this?" Menotti slowly looked around, as if expecting to see something unpleasant. "Maybe Blind Lady ain't in her right mind?" His breath went in with a snake-like hiss. "We know the Creep ain't. Maybe her and him planned to hook up somewhere and split the diamonds."

"Bad Man pops hubby and then they ride off into the sunset?"

"Exactly what I was thinking."

"Not a chance, Tio."

"Don't say that, Baby. There's chances on everything. Just check the internet." The burly man took another puff on his cigar. "Just the other day, I read about this woman who was changing herself into a man—battle gear and all."

Zeeman smiled at his partner, the lines of fatigue on his face momentarily disappearing. "She sounds like the ultimate optimist."

"All's I'm sayin' is, we gotta' take everything with a kernel of corn."

"You mean, grain of salt."

"That, too." Menotti gave his partner a questioning look. "With Popovitch in custody, what do we do about getting revenge for him killing Meri?"

"Nothing. He did us a favor."

"That don't sound like you, Baby."

"Meri suckered me," Zeeman explained.

"I don't get you."

"Meri wasn't pressured into killing Blind Lady. Popovitch was her lover." An angry shadow passed over the tall man's face. "The two of them planned to kill his wife for the insurance, and then get married. She got us involved to protect her from Bad Man until he could be framed for Blind Lady's murder."

"But, the doll…"

"The doll's real. So are the diamonds." Zeeman cleared his throat. "The truth is, she and Popovitch were going to return it to Kandinsky and place the blame on Bad Man for its theft."

"But how could they frame the Creep?"

"Meri had been intimate with Bad Man. So there'd have been no trouble adding his DNA to Blind Lady's corpse. They wouldn't have to worry about him following because Kandinsky would kill Bad Man in retaliation for taking the doll." His lips drew a little closer together. "You and I would end up dead, or flat broke."

"I said we shouldn't trust Meri." Menotti thrust a finger at his partner. "You remember I said we shouldn't trust her."

"I remember." Zeeman tilted his head toward the main house. "What were you doing in there?"

"Looking for the doll."

"The old man's in there. Didn't he wonder why you were tossing the place?"

"I flashed the Lieutenant's badge I used when you, me and Meri were grifting. He put up no complaint."

Zeeman squared his shoulders, turning toward the beach. "Did the old man know about the doll?"

"Not a clue. Kept muttering how his son never played with dolls even when he was a kid." Menotti flicked the ash from his cigar. "How'd the cops get to Popovitch so fast?"

"Blind Lady."

The burly man gave his partner a startled look. "She ratted out her husband?"

"Considering what her husband had planned, can you fault the woman?"

"Even so… I thought she was—you know—a kitten."

"Kittens have claws." Zeeman checked his watch. Then he stamped his feet against the chill. "Too cold to stand out all night."

"Did you get a room?"

"Top floor. Twin beds. Overlooks the road."

"Let's go."

"I registered as a single."

"I'll tell the old man you're helping me with a stakeout on another suspect in Meri's murder. He won't kick about me staying the night, in your room."

Zeeman suddenly turned toward the cabin. "I just had a brainstorm, Tio."

"I've been tellin' you for years 'bout the value of a rethink."

"Charlie Owens."

Menotti gave his partner a confused stare. "And that would be?"

"Owens works here. The local law showed up while I was registering. I ducked out but hung around to listen." Zeeman glanced toward the ocean. "He's the reason I found out the truth about Meri. Owens is a big fan of Sydney Popovitch."

"Everybody's entitled to critics and fans. But, I don't see how this gets us anywhere."

"Somebody in this town has the doll. It's not Blind Lady. It's not Popovitch's old man. I think Owens is our best bet."

The burly man frowned down at his wet shoes. "Do you know where Owens lives?"

"No." Zeeman lifted his chin slightly, toward the main house. "But, the old man'll have the address."

"That still leaves the problem of getting to Owens." The burly man raised his eyes to his partners. "Too late to rent a car."

"Flash the badge. Tell the old boy we need to borrow his Caddy."

Chapter 12
"A Clue to the Doll's Location"

The windows, in the colonial-style house that provided Charlie Owens with an address, were dark. The glass-plate rectangles cast a foreboding aura, not unlike that of unused coffins. Behind the white frame structure was a two-story garage. Its top level provided living quarters. Access to the upper story was by way of a wooden staircase mounted to the garage's wall. Two small square windows there were fitted with venetian-style blinds. Dim light filtered through the slats suggesting the promise of occupant wakefulness. Snow was falling thick and hard.

"You're certain Charlie Owens lives there?" Zeeman asked as he parked Jerome Popovitch's Cadillac on the street in front of the house.

"That's what the old man said," replied Menotti. "He's got the flop above the garage. His parents own the house." The burly man hesitated, still staring at the garage. "How do you want to play this?"

"Owens knows me as Mike North, from Arizona."

Menotti's eyebrows shot up, as he turned toward his partner. "Wasn't that careless?"

"I hadn't planned on dealing with him at the time."

"All's I'm sayin' is, Owens'll be a loose end. He'll point the cops to us after we leave. That much trouble we don't need."

"He won't talk. He's too involved with Popovitch."

"You mean the doll?"

"Charlie Owens knows more about Meri's murder than he told the local law. If he says anything about us, I'll see that he finds himself in the tank with Popovitch."

"Baby, that's all well and good but we'd be in there with him. How do we get the diamonds if that happens?"

"Relax, Tio." Zeeman motioned toward the garage. "I'll handle this alone. If something goes sour you deal with Blind Lady for the Bling-blings."

Menotti screwed up his face. "I'd better come in with you."

"There's no need."

"Baby, you know how you get when you get how you get."

"It won't happen."

"I believe you. But we can't afford to have this gig to bite us in the ass."

Zeeman shut off the car engine, still watching the garage. "You got your handcuffs?"

"Sure I got my cuffs."

"Then we'll chain the kid to something before we leave. That'll keep him shut until we get out of town."

"Assuming he's got the Bling-blings and assuming somebody don't come by and find him handcuffed." Menotti scratched his cheek. "You think Owen's is still up?"

"Lights make it seem so."

"House looks dark." Menotti eyed the structures, slightly uneasy. "Could be everybody's in bed in there. Could be everybody's out." He looked over at Zeeman. "What if they are out and they come back while you and me are in the midst of get Owens to tells us about the doll?"

"Wait in the car. I'll take care of it."

"No need for that." Menotti hesitated. "You want my knucks?"

"The kid's a creampuff."

The burly man twisted in one direction and then the other, looking at the surrounding area. "We'll probably have to gag him."

"So we'll gag him."

"He might start kickin' stuff." Menotti let out his breath in a sigh. "Neighbors could hear, and come over. We'll probably have to tie his feet."

"So, we'll tie his feet."

"'Course, he could start bumping up and down, too."

"What are you suggesting, Tio? That I kill Owens?"

"'Course not, Baby." The burly man gave his partner a nervous, sidelong look. "Not if you don't want to."

"I don't want to."

The two men watched the garage's upper story windows in silence for several long moments, hoping to see some indication of occupancy.

"What if Owens got the doll, like you figure, only he's put it someplace?" Menotti asked.

"A guy living above his parent's garage doesn't have extras for hiding places."

"Maybe Popovitch slipped him a few bucks for a rented hidey-hole?"

Zeeman glared at his partner. "Don't you ever think upbeat?"

"Baby, I gotta' keep my options open."

A silhouette crossed in front of one of the lighted windows.

"Looks like Owens is still up," Zeeman said.

Menotti sniffed wetly. "At least we won't interrupt his sleep."

"When did you start caring about us interrupting anybody's sleep?"

"Baby, ain't nothin' worse than dragging a guy outa' bed who's been sleepin' rough." The burly man shivered. "Hate getting' an eyeful of another guy's junk."

"What about a woman dragged out of bed in the rough?" Zeeman winked at his partner. "Anything wrong with female junk?"

"That I wouldn't mind. But, whenever women are involved in our gigs, they drag you *into* bed."

"That only happened once."

"Once, my ass. I've spent more time in hallways, listening to screaming bed springs, than the average roach."

"It happened once."

Menotti looked at his partner. "Frankly, I'm surprised that you and Blind Lady haven't been all over the place, in the rough, doing stuff people do in the rough, which I hardly never get to do."

"I don't get involved with married women."

"Yeah, like that never happened."

Again, Zeeman gave his partner a questioning stare.

"Mrs. Peterson, remember?" Menotti said.

"Never heard of her."

"We mowed her grass. Or, at least, I did."

"Grass?"

"When we was in Junior High."

Zeeman frowned, thinking back, and then grinned. "Ah, that Mrs. Peterson."

"Yeah, *that* Mrs. Peterson. I'm surprised you ain't got her name tattooed some place."

"Tio, she was strictly business."

"Then why did I do all the lawn-mowing while you spent the whole time inside with her?"

"She had a bush in need of tending."

"Bush my ass."

Zeeman grinned to himself, cocking an eyebrow. "I'm telling you, Tio, I had all I could do to keep that bush happy."

"You spent the whole afternoon on one lousy bush?"

"I did what I had to do."

"Sometimes it got to be a hundred and fourteen in the sun when I was mowing." Menotti's face puckered with painful memories. "My brain nearly fried. That's probably why I went bald." The burly man jabbed a finger at his partner. "You still got a full head of hair."

"What are you complaining about?" Zeeman stifled a laugh. "I didn't get a moment's rest"

"On one bush?"

"How many times, when you were mowing, did you stop and cool down?"

"Every little while."

"Well, while you were resting I was getting the life drained out of me."

"On one bush?"

"Tio, I had all I could handle."

The burly man hesitated, remembering back. "Well, maybe I do remember you being wore out every time we left her place."

Zeeman made an amused gesture of denial. "What with her husband overseas, and him loving that bush more than anything else, she wanted to be sure that it was properly tended during his absence."

Menotti gave his partner a piteous look. "I'm sorry I brought it up."

"It was a long time ago, Tio. I say we forget it."

"Thanks, Baby."

The tall man opened the car door. "Let's get this done."

The two men climbed from the car and quietly shut the vehicle's doors.

"You lead," said Menotti. "I'll follow."

The pair crept toward the garage along the snow-covered driveway. When they reached the wooden stairs to the upper level, the two men stopped.

"Them planks'll make noise," Menotti observed.

"I'll take my time."

"Hold it a second." Menotti pointed to the telephone line junction box mounted to the side of the garage. "I'll cut the line."

"Let it go."

"What do you mean, let it go?"

"These days, punks like Owens only have cell-phones."

Zeeman headed up the stairs. With each step up the riser the plank beneath the tall man's foot creaked, slightly. Menotti stepped back far enough to watch the windows in order to observe if Owens looked out in response to the noise.

At the top landing, Zeeman stopped and looked down. He waved one hand to signal Menotti.

The burly man went over to the stairs and made his way up, each step slow and careful.

After both men were side by side, Menotti crept over to the door, pressed one ear to it and listened. After a few seconds, he stepped back and nodded.

Zeeman stepped in front of his partner and knocked.

"Who is it?" a boyish voice called from the other side.

"Sid Popovitch," Zeeman returned, muffling his voice with one hand. "My lawyer busted me out."

Hurried footfalls announced Owens's arrival at the door. A lock clicked. Then the door swung inward.

"Man, I thought you were…" Owens began.

Zeeman forced the young man back into a single-room flat. He and Menotti rushed inside.

The space had a plastered ceiling with a parallel series of inset electrical fixtures to provide lighting. There were several upholstered chairs, a futon bed, a bureau, a toilet area and a kitchenette.

"Mike North!" Owens retreated. "What's this all about, man?"

"A doll stuffed with Bling-blings," Zeeman returned, as he went over to the young man.

Menotti kicked the door shut. "You remember that doll Sydney Popovitch gave you, Punk?"

"I don't know what you're talking about, man." The young man's head whipped from side to side, his eyes going from man to man. "Oh, shit."

"We'll wait," Zeeman returned.

"Sid described you guys. He wanted to know if I'd seen Mike Zeeman and Tio Menotti in Hull. You're Mike Zeeman and Tio Menotti."

"Ain't you the clever one, Punk."

"The doll, Charlie," Zeeman growled. "Give me the doll and we'll go."

"You guys got it wrong, man. Sid—Sid never gave me no doll."

"Hard or easy, Punk." Menotti took out his brass knuckles and slipped them on. "It's up to you and your dentist."

Owens backed away in terror. "Man, I don't want no trouble."

"Then give us the doll, Charlie."

"I'm tellin' you, man…"

"Stop stalling, Punk." Menotti slapped the brass knuckles into his palm. "Popovitch gave you the doll. I know it. You know it. And this great big mean man knows it." His bulldog face spread into a cruel grin. "You can hand it over. Or Baby, here, will kick you into next week."

Zeeman lunged forward and grabbed Owens by the shirt collar.

"Wait." Owens screamed. "Look, man, all I did was do a guy a favor."

"Tell us about the favor."

"Sid mailed me the doll. He wanted me to hide it. But it ain't here."

Zeeman offered the young man a lethal grin. "For some reason I don't believe you, Charlie."

"You have to, man!"

"Since when, Punk?"

"Look, man, Sid told me to put it in the cabin."

"What cabin?" Menotti demanded.

"The one him and Deidre were gonna' use."

"You're lying, Charlie. I searched the cabin."

"I swear, man. I left the doll in the bedroom for Meri. If it ain't there, I don't know what she did with it."

"You'd better not be shining me on, Punk," Menotti warned.

"Sure."

"I've talked to Mrs. Popovitch," Zeeman said sharply. "She says she doesn't have it."

"She's lying, man."

"What do you think, Baby?"

Zeeman swung a hard right, the tall man's fist striking Owens's chin, sending the kid skidding across the floor.

"How you like them apples, Punk?" Menotti smirked. "Next time Baby'll wear knucks. You'll end up with a busted jaw and maybe your eyeballs popped out. Get where I'm coming from, Punk?"

"I get it, man. And I wanna' keep my eyeballs where they are." Owens rubbed the swollen spot on his jaw, cowering on the floor. "But, I can't give you what I ain't got."

"I don't think he saw your knucks, Tio."

"For the love of god let me talk to Deidre!" Owens pushed the air in front of him with both hands. "I'll make her tell you."

Menotti flashed the brass on his hands. "Baby's losing patience."

Zeeman went over to Owens, jerked the young man up, and swung another hard right; his huge fist catching the young man on the side of his skull.

Owens flew sideways; bouncing against a wall before sprawling on the floor, unconscious.

"My nose says you got his attention, Baby." The burly man made a disgusted face. "Punk, there, shit his pants."

Owens grunted something and tried to sit up. Then he flopped back down, and lay still.

Zeeman and Menotti stepped forward, eying the fallen man.

"What do you think, Tio?"

"Baby, he might be telling the truth. Then, again, he might not. This is a tough call."

"I think he's lying." Zeeman stared at Owens for several moments. "Blind Lady's cabin has three rooms: bedroom, bath and front room. The kitchenette and dining area are in the main part. No doll."

"You couldn't have been too thorough without Blind Lady tumblin' over something."

"I didn't miss it, Tio."

"Then, why lie to about it?"

Zeeman shook his head. "I know I didn't miss it."

"Just for grins, let's pretend that Owens told the truth. Where could she have hidden it?"

"I searched from attic to cupboards."

"What about in a wall?"

"Tourist cabins aren't built with sliding wall panels in mind."

Menotti pointed down at Owens. "You heard him. He said she had it."

"He said she knew where it was."

The burly man gave Owens a nudge with a shoe. The young man didn't make a sound.

"You killed him, Baby."

"I didn't hit him that hard."

"Not that I'm complainin'. Now, we won't have to worry about him callin' the cops. But you shoulda' got him to tell us where he'd hid the doll before he died."

Zeeman squatted and touched the young man's neck. "Relax, Tio. Charlie's still alive."

"Oh, yeah. I see him breathing."

"You sound disappointed."

"To be honest, I've got mixed emotions."

"Let's toss this place, just to be sure it's not here."

For the next twenty minutes Menotti and Zeeman methodically searched the small living space. They found half a kilo of cocaine and a huge roll of rubberbanded cash beneath a floorboard. Two kilos of marijuana were concealed by a sliding wall panel. But, no doll.

"This Punk is really pissing me off!" the burly man roared.

"It isn't here, Tio. Charlie claims Blind Lady has it. So, my search or not, it's time to chat with her."

Barely conscious, Owens clawed his way across the floor until he reached a wall. Then he flopped over onto his back and pushed with his heels until his body slid up the wall leaving him in a seated position. His eyes bulged. His mouth bled.

"Don't hit me no more." His expression was desperate. "Please don't hit me no more."

"Was the doll in something when you hid it in the cabin?"

"I tucked in up under the springs in the rocker."

Menotti gave his partner a look. "You check there?"

"I tilted it to one side."

"It's above the bottom mesh hiding the springs."

Menotti carried the illegal substances over to where Owens sat, and dropped them at the young man's feet. "Killing him would be a big problem solver, Baby."

"I won't say nothing, man," the young man whimpered.

"How much cash, Tio?" Zeeman asked.

"Nearly twelve grand, Baby."

"You can have it," Owens said. He wiped at the blood dribbling from his mouth, his terrified eyes on Zeeman. "Just let me live, okay?"

"What do you think, Baby?"

"Could be, we let him live. Could be, we break his legs at the knees to make sure he isn't lying. I can't decide."

"I'm telling you the truth," Owens sobbed. "I swear to god, I'm telling the truth."

The burly man pocketed the cash. "If you're lying, we'll be back." He rubbed his hands together. "Baby, has this thing about liars. Can't control himself. You'll be dead if that happens."

Zeeman addressed Charlie Owens with, "Did Popovitch say anything about Meri Darling?"

"Sid said she was coming to Hull," Owens replied. "Said, Meri'd be staying overnight at Pop's. Sid said to give her any help she needed." He wiped the blood from his face. "But, she got killed. Then, Sid got arrested." He started to cry. "Everything's goin' down the shitter, man, and all I did was do a guy a favor."

"You buy this, Baby?"

"Those aren't crocodile tears." Zeeman pointed to the stove in the kitchenette. "Cuff him to the handle."

"I said I wouldn't talk," Owens pleaded.

"We'll point the locals here after we get the doll," Zeeman returned. "They'll turn you loose."

"But they'll see my stash, man."

Menotti breathed in between his teeth. "Tough times call for tough measures, Punk."

Chapter 13
"Tying Loose Ends"

Snow was falling in thick, fat flakes when Menotti and Zeeman parked Jerome's car in the drive, fronting the resort. The white downpour turned to slush, as it hit the brown grass. The wind was blowing hard, creating blizzard conditions.

Zeeman climbed out of the Cadillac, followed by Menotti. Then both men headed for the cabins.

"Baby, you weren't supposed to beat the Punk half to death."

"I tapped him, Tio."

The burly man gave his partner a shocked look. "Well, I hope to God you ain't gonna' tap Blind Lady."

Zeeman's face flushed with irritation.

"I won't touch her, okay?"

"But you know how you get when you get how you get. Especially, after somebody lies to you."

"I know how I get."

The burly man eyed his partner askance. "You know why you lost control with Owens?"

"I know why. He lied to me."

"That's one reason. But, the other reason is because Blind Lady's a looker."

"You've lost me, Tio."

"Baby, we both saw she was a looker." Menotti coughed and cleared his throat, self-consciously. "Nice legs. Nice face. Nice in between. I can understand you gettin' tempted."

"I wasn't tempted."

Menotti stared upwards, his eyes squinting against the falling snow, as if trying to form his thoughts into words. "Baby, any guy could get tempted. And a guy who gets tempted might think serious 'bout what happens when there's temptations." His eyes returned to his partner. "Baby, you gotta' let Blind Lady go."

"There's nothing to let go, Tio. I spoke with Deidre for ten minutes. How much could be going on after ten minutes?"

"So it's Deidre, now?"

The tall man let out his breath in a long sigh. "Back off, Tio."

"All's I'm sayin' is, when it comes to you and women, ten minutes is all it takes."

"If you think I'm not holding up my end, then it's time we went our separate ways."

"I'm not talkin' 'bout bustin' up the partnership."

"Forget it."

The two men continued to within a few yards of the cabin nearest the beach, and then stopped.

"Baby, I got rules against puttin' heat on blind ladies."

Zeeman shifted his stance slightly. "Since when?"

"Since my grandma went blind from them allergies."

"That old crone drank anything with or without a proof marker. That's why she went blind."

"She had cravings 'cause of a vitamin deficiency. People with cravings tipple."

"Yeah, Tio, I remember her tippling."

The burly man cocked an eyebrow. "All's I'm sayin', Baby, is you'll have to deal with Blind Lady. I can't do it."

"She'll come to terms."

The burly man wiped the falling wet from the top of his head. "How?"

"I'll do what I have to do, Tio."

"Well in the meantime, I'm out here freezin' my balls." Menotti jerked his thumb at the cabin. "She's in there toasty warm, without balls." The burly man looked around for a few seconds. Then, he gave a grumbling shrug. "How long's it gonna' take?"

"No more than ten minutes."

Menotti looked at his partner for a long moment. Then he said, "Maybe we need to offer her two-thirds on the split? You know. To avoid any problems. What do you think?"

The tall man reached out and gave his partner a pat on the shoulder.

"Just the same, Baby, maybe you should mention how them Bling-blings are illegal, which they are, and how it could mean jail time if she takes a cut."

"Why would I do that?"

"That way, she might not want her cut."

A shadowy figure clothed in black, slightly built with blinking lights on his foil cap, came out the main house. The sound of his footsteps descending the slushy steps caught the attention of Zeeman and Menotti.

Zeeman grabbed his partner by the arm. "Look what arrived."

"It's the Creep," Menotti murmured. Then a greedy grin lifted his eyebrows. "Bonus time, Baby."

"I want to be sure he whacked Kandinsky."

"The Russian's will pay regardless. They want him dead."

"Why?"

"My contact said they were restructuring."

Zeeman watched Steiner's meandering, paranoid approach, carefully keeping his face expressionless. "I want to be sure."

"Baby, this ain't like you."

"I'm seeing things differently, that's all."

"It's Blind Lady. Baby, you ain't been the same since you first saw her."

"You get the fuckin' doll?" Steiner demanded

"We're discussing possibilities, Creep," Menotti returned when Steiner drew near. Then the burly man looked at his partner. "Baby, I'm thinkin' we blow off that proof thingy."

"What the fuck d'you mean by possibilities?"

"There are possibilities and then there are possibilities, Creep."

Steiner crossed his arms defiantly, his eyes darting back and forth from man to man. "Where's the doll?"

"We don't know, Bad Man."

"Didn't you talk to Sydney-Boy?"

"Popovitch is in jail."

"What the fuck for?"

"Cops think he killed Meri, Bad Man." The tall man's mouth turned down at the corners. "With him behind bars, our deal went south."

"Leon, shut the fuck up!" Steiner glared toward the beach. "This ain't no dead deal." Then he turned his glare at Zeeman. "Sydney-Boy being in the tank don't change shit, Mr. Zeeman. The Bitch has the doll."

The tall man jabbed Steiner with a stiff finger. "How's Kandinsky, Bad Man?"

"The shit-bag took a fall." Steiner shrugged, sneering. "Leon says he was overdue."

"Meaning you did the hit on him?"

"Not me, Mr. Zeeman. Leon. Leon don't like guys who get in our way."

"You hear that, Baby?"

Zeeman nodded. "Ka-ching, Tio."

"Hey, Creep. As long as you're tellin' glory tales, who else got in the way?"

"You mean Vasiliev, Menotti? Leon gave the fuckin' bastard what he had comin'."

"We're thinking about Meri, Bad Man."

Steiner lifted his shoulders in an exaggerated shrug. "That cunt knew better than to cross me."

"So you killed her?" Zeeman said between his teeth.

"Leon did what had to be done, Mr. Zeeman." The little man glanced to his right. "Ain't that right, Leon?"

"Popovitch has the doll, Creep," Menotti growled, shaking with rage. "Those were your words. So, why kill Meri?"

"As Nietzsche said, 'It is hard enough to remember my opinions, without also remembering my reasons for them.'"

Zeeman put his right hand into his coat pocket and gripped his revolver. "Go talk to Mrs. Popovitch, Tio. Bad Man and I have business."

"Not so fast, Baby." Menotti forced his way between the men.

Steiner, suddenly alarmed, stepped wide of the partners. "You guys haven't talked to the Bitch?"

"Questions were asked, Creep. Answers were given. We're still mulling."

"Well mull this, Menotti. You and your candy-ass pal couldn't take cookies from a jar." Steiner looked from one to the other. "Time for me and Leon to step up."

"Blind Lady doesn't have the doll, Bad Man." Zeeman said between his teeth.

"The Bitch has it if I say she has it." Steiner jutted his chin toward Deidre's cabin. "Leon and me'll boogie her 'till the doll dances out." He made an obscene slurping sound. "Ain't the right, Leon?"

"You're paying us to get the doll, Creep," the burly man said, moving obliquely to cut off any approach Steiner might make to Deidre's cabin.

"You had your chance, Menotti."

"If you're taking over, Creep, pay up."

Steiner cleared his throat, then cleared it again. "You don't get shit 'till I get the doll."

Zeeman crowded over. "What were you doing in the house, Bad Man?"

"Old man Popovitch said a cop searched the dump." Steiner forced a worried grin at Zeeman, retreating a step. "Even borrowed his car." The little man gave out a hollow laugh. "You waving a badge, Menotti?"

"How is it Old man Popovitch turned glib, Bad Man?"

The little man made a long, wet snort and swallowed. "I got my winning ways, Mr. Zeeman."

"How winning, Creep?"

"According to Nietzsche, 'That which does not kill us makes us stronger.'" Steiner grinned. "That old man was not destined for strength."

"You hear that, Baby?"

"There was no need to kill him, Bad Man."

"Tying loose ends, Mr. Zeeman." The little man started toward the cabin. "Time me and Leon got acquainted with the Bitch."

Zeeman grabbed Steiner by the arm. "You're not going anywhere."

Steiner jerked free.

Again, Menotti rushed between the two men. "Baby, have another talk with Mrs. Popovitch." Zeeman offered Steiner an icy grin. "Bad Man and me'll confab on a backup plan, if she don't come across."

"Tio…" Zeeman looked at his partner, the vengeance in his eyes replaced by concern.

"I'm gonna' have to insist, Baby."

Zeeman slowly nodded. "I'm with you." He closed the distance to Menotti. Then, he secretly slipped the pistol into the burly man's coat pocket. "Point by point, Tio."

"No problem, Baby." Menotti patted the pocket containing the gun. "Even if it takes six tries, I'll get them points through his head." The burly man gave Steiner a plastic smile. "Come on, Creep. Let's you and me and Leon put our heads together over Blind Lady." He slipped his fingers beneath the lapels of his jacket and sloughed it higher on his shoulders. "And when we get done talkin', I'm gonna' show you something that'll blow your mind."

"Mr. Zeeman. Tell the Bitch that if she don't come through, me and Leon are goin' in. And I mean goin' in deep. Ain't that right, Leon?"

Chapter 14
"Cutting a Deal"

Mike Zeeman trotted through the slush over to the cabin occupied by Deidre Popovitch. He pressed his ear to the door, but no sound came through the wood. The tall man tried the knob. It turned. He pushed it open, going inside, and then shutting it.

As when Zeeman had searched the cabin, the only light came from the fireplace. Flames licked and crackled around split logs within the box, warming the entire room. In spite of the burning wood, his nose caught the scent of melted wax mixed with that of Deidre's perfume: Sandalwood. He took out one of the candles the old man had given him and lit it with a lighter. As Zeeman dropped the lighter back into a pocket, he noticed two suitcases to one side of the door. He squatted, opened each and quickly rummaged through their contents. No doll. No diamonds. He closed the suitcases and then stood up.

"You made good time Serge," Deidre called out, from the bedroom. "I was worried you hadn't gotten my message." She tapped he way out into the front room, and over to the rocker. "Sorry I ruined your weekend. But, I'm in over my head." She took a deep breath. "Sydney's involved with people who'll kill me to get something he stole. I promise to make it worth your while. I just need help getting to the nearest airport." She hesitated, listening. "Serge?"

The blind woman had changed into dark slacks and red blouse. A fringed red shawl draped across narrow shoulders. The same fuzzy slippers encased her feet. Her posture was very straight and proper. Her hands hung by her sides, her knees were tightly together. Deidre's sightless eyes were wide open.

"It's Mike." Zeeman announced.

Surprised by his voice, Deidre's reached out and grabbed the rocker to steady herself. "Mr. Vasiliev's on his way." Her voice choked, barely above a whisper. "He'll be here any moment. He used to be with the KGB."

"Serge's not coming."

She wetted her lips several times. "Did you hurt him?"

"No." The tall man moved toward the blind woman holding the candle casually. "But, your friend's been shot."

In the dim light, he saw her skin go gray. "Serge's dead?"

"I don't know."

"Who did it?"

"Harry Steiner."

"Where?"

"Your apartment."

"I sent Serge there," Deidre said, her voice breaking. The blind woman felt her way in front of the chair and sat down, her entire body trembling. "How do you know this?"

"Steiner told me. He's proud of it."

There was a thin-lipped silence.

"Your name is Mike Zeeman," she said.

The tall man was taken aback for a moment. He tried to bluff with a denial.

"I'm blind, Mr. Zeeman. Not stupid." Deidre raised her chin, slightly, turning her head toward his voice. "You told me that you had been married to Meri Darling." The blind woman cleared her throat. "When I was at the police station speaking with the sheriff, he told me all about Meri Darling. She had been married only once. To you, Mike Zeeman."

"I'm embarrassed by my carelessness."

"A scary man like you, Mr. Zeeman, doesn't get embarrassed." The chair began rocking under the pressure of her legs. "What now?"

His chin dropped, his eyes staring at the dimly-lit floor. Not liking what he was hearing. Not liking that he had been outed. Not liking the fear she must be feeling for Vasiliev. Not liking the prospect of her tipping the police to his presence.

"Tell me something, Mr. Zeeman. Who jerks your chain?"

"Nobody."

His cheeks held a flush of color as his stare rose to her face.

"You work with Tio Menotti, another scary man," Deidre continued.

"Tio's a puppy."

The blind woman's fingers knotted into fists at the ends of the chair arms. "Did Serge get help?"

"Tio telephoned for an ambulance." The tall man's eyes darted to the crackling fireplace. "He doesn't know how it turned out."

"Why would Mr. Steiner shoot Serge?"

"That's how Steiner gets his jollies."

Her fingers flexed open and she rocked back and forth for many seconds, thinking. "Do you work for Mr. Steiner?"

"Tio and I work for ourselves. Your husband works for Steiner."

"Sydney says Mr. Steiner works for Mr. Kandinsky, a Russian mobster."

"Worked. Kandinsky's dead."

Her feet went flat on the floor, stopping the moving chair. "Accident?"

"Homicide."

"You?"

"Steiner."

Her rocking resumed.

"From what the police told me, Mr. Zeeman, there have been lots of scary people in your life." She bit her lip and staring straight ahead. "Most of those are now dead, none by natural causes. You're suspected in several of those murders, not to mention numerous extortions and countless incidental offenses."

"I blame it on a deprived childhood."

"Why do people with a criminal history always blame their childhood?"

"Because there are so many bleeding heart liberals willing to believe it."

Again the blind woman's tongue went across her lips. "You don't feel the least bit guilty?"

The tall man glanced back at the door, looking uneasy. "Do the police know I'm here?"

"Not from me." The rocking ceased, her feet flat on the floor. "But, they're looking for you. Is Mr. Steiner in Hull?"

"Just outside."

The rocker went still as she made an involuntary gasp.

"Do you know Steiner?" Zeeman asked.

"Sydney told me about him. Is Mr. Steiner schizophrenic?"

"I'm not an expert on such things." He studied Deidre with genuine interest. "But, Steiner talks to an invisible guy named Leon if that helps."

"That would fit. Does he think the world is out to get him?"

"In Steiner's case it really is."

"Schizophrenics often hallucinate," she observed. "They frequently hear voices, feel like their being touched, see things as well as people that are not there. It's a devastating disease." Her sightless eyes closed as she considered. "Paranoia often plays a prominent role. The sufferer is frequently terrified. It's not uncommon for schizophrenics to see blood running out of eyes: the eyes of people the schizophrenic believes to be evil." Deidre's unseeing eyes reopened and she drew in a breath. "Mr. Steiner may have removed his family's eyes in order to destroy that which the sufferer perceives as evil." She smiled softly. "I'm surprised that he would associate with you or Mr. Menotti. The two of you must look, to him, like evil incarnate."

"Would you like me to bring Steiner in?"

"I'd rather you didn't."

His lips curled faintly, amused by her. "Let's talk about Bling-blings, shall we?"

"Sydney refused to tell me where he'd hidden the doll."

"Mrs. Popovitch, you're playing me."

"We've been playing each other, Mr. Zeeman." The chair resumed moving back and forth, creating a soft squeaking sound. "Now that we're done playing, what's our agenda for tonight?"

"You're going to give me the doll."

She let go a jerky little laugh. "I don't have it."

"Charlie Owens says otherwise."

"Charlie's a drug dealer. Surely, lying isn't beneath him?"

"Tio and I made sure he wasn't lying."

Again her feet went flat on the floor, stopping the rocker. "Is Charlie alive?"

"He was when Tio and I left." The tall man hesitated. "As the police told you, I'm a scary guy. Give me the doll. I'll go away."

"The truth is, I burned the doll." Deidre tilted her head toward the heat from the fireplace. "See for yourself."

Zeeman strode over to the fire. The flames were lapping on the pipe-frame of a large doll. The clothing, head and body padding were nothing but ash.

"Diamonds don't burn." Zeeman glanced over at her. "They'll sink to the bottom of the ash."

"There were no diamonds. The doll was empty." The blind woman pointed in the direction of the fireplace. "Pop said there was a shovel among the fireplace tools. Scoop up the ashes. See for yourself."

He returned to the chair. "I smelled melted wax when I arrived."

"Residue in the doll's frame."

"Stop lying," he returned, sharply.

"I'm not." She raised her dark eyebrows. "I found the doll on the bed where Charlie had left it. But its body had already been cut open." She nodded slightly, lips grimacing. "The frame was still inside. But it's empty, its end-caps gone." The rocking resumed. "Sydney's probably swallowed a million dollars worth of diamonds."

Zeeman wagged his dark head. "I don't buy it."

"You offered me half a million for the Bling-blings. How would I benefit myself by lying to you?"

Zeeman tilted the lighted candle over the table in front of the furnishing, dribbled a puddle of wax, and then set the candle into the molten mire. "I think a clever Blind Lady, like you, could cut the frame from the doll. Melting the wax would be easy enough. Just set the frame atop a stove burner." He made a slight gesture. "A little pouring. A little scooping. A little bagging." He shrugged his broad shoulders. "A million in Bling-blings all in one bundle."

"But, I would still have to sell them. Who knows what an inexperienced person like me would receive? You, on the other hand, offered me an acceptable figure."

His words came out through stiff lips. "Don't underestimate me, Mrs. Popovitch."

A dog barked outside, some distance away. The blind woman jerked her head toward the sound, as if it was a warning.

"Deidre." She smiled in the direction of his voice. "We've talked. I made you laugh." The rocking stopped. "Whether you want to admit it or not, Mike, we've become friends."

"All right, Deidre. But in my world friends don't lie to each other."

The blind woman shifted in the rocker as though she could not find a comfortable position. "All right, the truth is the Bling-blings are worth a million and that's what I want for them."

"You won't get away from Hull without my approval." His voice was low and ominous.

"Meaning you're willing to kill me?"

"Meaning I'll do what I have to."

"Now that Mr. Kandinsky is dead, they're mine."

"If I leave here empty-handed, your next visitor will be Harry Steiner. Is that what you want?"

"You wouldn't."

"After he rapes you. After he tortures you. You'll point him to the Bling-blings. He'll get them. Then, he'll kill you." The tall man's mouth turned down at the corners. "I'll be outside waiting for him. I'll take the Bling-blings from Steiner. I'll kill him. Then, I'll disappear with the booty." Zeeman tilted toward her. "Let's come to terms. I'll split the sale proceeds equally with you. I'll take care of Steiner so that he'll never bother you again."

The blind woman considered for several seconds. "You offered half a million dollars. Cash?"

"I don't have the cash. I won't until the diamonds are sold."

"That's hardly equitable."

"Life isn't fair, Deidre. No matter what happens, I'll end up with the diamonds. My way you'll end up a wealthy woman."

Her shoulders moved, vaguely. "How do I know I can trust you?"

"You don't. But your husband's words about Steiner should convince you that I'm the lesser of two evils. Give me the diamonds. I'll sell them. I'll come back. I'll give you the promised share."

She offered his voice a bleak smile. "That would still leave Mr. Steiner."

"I'll take care of Steiner before I leave. If you want proof, I'll let you listen while I snap his neck."

"I'd rather not."

"Well?"

"How do I know you won't leave me to Mr. Steiner after I give you the Bling-blings?"

The muscles in the tall man's jaw rippled. "Steiner is dead no matter how this plays out between you and me."

Her eyebrows shot up. "Would he still be dead if we settled on me getting two-thirds of the sale price?"

"Don't be greedy." Zeeman squared his broad shoulders. "The offer is half." The skin across his face tensed, his lips thinned. For several seconds he remained silent, thinking, remembering. Then he said, "Don't make this tougher than it has to be."

"I want two-thirds. Give me two-thirds and we have a deal."

"This isn't a classroom exercise." The tall man reached down, grabbed her shoulders, and jerked Deidre to her feet. "There's a madman outside. He killed Meri. He shot your friend, Vasiliev. And he killed your father-in-law."

"Pop?"

"He's dead." Zeeman gave her a shake.

The blind woman winced in pain. "Mike, you're hurting me."

"It's nothing to what Steiner will dish out." Zeeman eased her back into the chair and backed away. "Agree to my offer, Deidre."

"Why did he kill Pop?"

"Steiner said he was tying up loose ends." The tall man's voice resumed its soft cooing. "Don't worry. I'll handle Steiner. We'll catch the ferry to Boston. We'll go to the diamond district tomorrow. By tomorrow night you'll have a nice bank balance and I'll be out of your life."

"Men aren't wired to keep promises. You'll take the lot and I'll never see you again."

Zeeman bent down and kissed her forehead. "Enjoy your time with Steiner." Then he turned and headed for the door.

Deidre got to her feet, her arms extended in a pleading gesture. "Mike, wait."

There was a short span of silence, during which the dog gave out another howl.

"I'm all out of time and patience, Deidre."

"I took the Bling-blings from the doll, like you said." The blind woman pinched up her face, as if the truth hurt. "I put them in a pillowcase. I tied the pillowcase to the springs in the rocker's seat." She gestured slightly with her hands. "You'll find it above the first layer of padding." She pursed her lips together. "You'll keep your word?"

That tall man smiled, but not cordially. "I always do."

"You must be God's second gift."

Zeeman walked back to the rocker and took Deidre's hands. He pulled her clear of the furnishing. Quickly, he tipped the furnishing onto its side. After squatting down he rummaged around among the chair-springs for a few seconds. Eventually, Zeeman located the pillowcase. After removing it from the chair, he rose, up-righted the chair, and assisted Deidre's return to it. Then he opened the cloth sack. Inside were hundreds of faceted diamonds, still dulled by the wax. The Bling-blings rattled softly, within the cloth, like tiny marbles.

"I'm blind, Mr. Zeeman. I have no job. I'm divorcing a husband who wants me dead." A shadow of desperation crossed the Deidre's face. "If I can't get another job, I'll spend the rest of my days on Social Security." A tightness pulled down the corners of her mouth. "I don't like taking handouts. Please consider that, once you've sold those diamonds."

Zeeman tucked the bag into his coat pocket. Then he picked up the candle and walked over to cabin door. When he reached it, Zeeman had one of his rare moments of pity. He looked back at the blind woman. Deidre had resumed rocking, her face pale with despair.

Zeeman opened the door. "Deidre, you won't have to worry about..."

There was a soft popping sound. Then, Zeeman sagged backward falling onto the slush-covered ground, outside the cabin.

"Won't have to worry about what?" Deidre said. "Mike?" Her voice arched, strained and high. "Why won't I worry?"

Chapter 15
"Steiner and the Blind Lady"

A moment later, Harry Steiner stepped into the cabin. The flashlight in his right hand up-lit his bruised and cut face, giving it a ghostly quality. His jaw looked like a rotten plum. His left eye resembled an overripe, bursting avocado. Fresh blood dripped, like cherry syrup, from his nose. He smiled with teeth like salted peanuts. The little man closed the door and rolled the flashlight's bluish beam around the room.

"'Ah, women,'" declared Steiner. "'They make the highs higher and the lows more frequent.'" Steiner swung the light over to the blind woman. "What're your thoughts on Nietzsche, Mrs. Popovitch?"

"He was a mental case," she returned, tilting forward in the chair. There was a nervous quiver to her voice. "Who... who are you?"

"Harry Steiner."

Deidre went white; her voice shrill. "Mike!"

"Zeeman and Menotti are dead, Mrs. Popovitch." The little man stroked his unlit foil cap, grinning. "We took 'em out, didn't we Leon?"

"No!" she screamed.

"Just you and me, now." The little man moved closer, washing the light beam up and down her body. "People fight like wild cats at the end. They scream. They claw. They spit." His eyes were fixed on Deidre: unblinking, beady, glittering with lust. "Even their teeth get in the act, unless all they're all gums like Vasiliev." Steiner shivered. "Nothin' worse than old man drool from a leg-gumming. Ain't that right, Leon?"

"Dear God," the blind woman groaned, sagging back into the chair.

"Take it from me, Bitch, God ain't even heard of this shit-hole." Steiner leered at her. "I'm sure Sydney-Boy talked 'bout me." The little man stopped and made an obscene sucking noise, his gaze moving back and forth across her. "I'm what you might call a special person: gifted, if you like." He twisted to the left and yelled, "I don't need no more ass-wipe from you, Leon!" Then Steiner made a vague movement with the flashlight, sending shadows darting like running cats across the ceiling and down the walls; his eyes returned to her.

"You're as mad as a hatter." Deidre's face crumpled with terror, and then stiffened.

"I'm not a famous Steiner. You know, from the red planet." Steiner resumed his approach. "Those guys live in Poughkeepsie."

"What do you want, Mr. Steiner?"

"Surely, you jest, Bitch." He glanced to his right. "Tell her she jests, Leon."

"I jest quite often, because I enjoy it. But, at the moment I'm not in a jesting mood. I think it's the company I'm keeping."

"Nietzsche said, 'Between two absolutely different spheres, as between subject and object, there is no causality, no correctness, and no expression; there is, at most, an aesthetic relation.'" The little man stopped again, giving the room another wash of light. "That's what you and me got, Bitch. An aesthetic relation that pumps my prick." He made the slurping noise, again. "Nice tits."

"If you don't leave, I'll call the police."

"You won't be callin' anybody, Bitch, lessen' you hand over my doll."

"Your doll?" Deidre returned, her voice thick with sarcasm. "Sydney said it belonged to Mr. Kandinsky."

"He's dead, too."

"You, I presume?"

"Listen, Bitch, that was then and this is now. And my now ain't Kandinsky's now because he ain't around, now."

She squinted in disbelief. "I should think you'd find murder tiresome, Mr. Steiner."

"I do. But, Leon loves it." He giggled maniacally, stamping his foot repeatedly with glee. "Leon really ventilated Kandinsky. By the time it was done, Kandinsky could piss from both ends."

"Your humor eludes me."

"Well, I guess you had to be there." The little man's face twisted into a macabre grin. "What size are them milkers?"

The blind woman gave a small, defeated shrug. "Logic dictates that you're going to kill me no matter what I do."

Steiner whirled to the right shouting, "Nobody's s'posed to tell her, Leon! It was supposed to be a big secret."

"Logic also dictates that I have nothing to lose by keeping you from your goal."

He turned back toward her and considered for a moment. Then his face brightened. "Leon lied."

"I don't think that's possible."

"I ain't gonna' kill you. All I want is the doll." He resumed his approach. "Here's the deal, Bitch. You give me the doll. I'll leave. Simple, huh?" He glanced over one shoulder. "Tell her how simple it is, Leon. And don't fuck it up, this time by telling her what's really gonna' happen."

Deidre leaned over one side of the chair and fumbled along the floor until her fingers touched her handbag. The blind woman picked it up and set it on her lap. From within, she withdrew her cellular phone.

"What the fuck are you doin'?" Steiner demanded. "Ask her what the fuck's she's doin', Leon!"

"I'm calling the police, Mr. Steiner."

He rushed over, jerked the phone from Deidre's grasp, then tossed it across the room, shattering the plastic device against a wall.

"You don't do shit, Bitch, 'lessen I tell you to do shit!"

Once more defeated, Deidre dropped her purse to the floor. "My husband's on his way."

"As Nietzsche once said, 'Every concept arises from the equation of unequal things.'" The little man watched her stonily. "And that, Bitch, means my equal ain't fuckin' 'round with your unequal, when your unequal's lyin' to get me by the balls." He tilted toward her, his chin jutting out with contempt. "Sydney-Boy's ass is locked in the tank at Boston P.D."

"His lawyer's arranged bail."

"No, he ain't."

"Yes he has."

Steiner backed away, uneasily. From the look on the little man's face he was partially convinced by her lie.

"Gimme' the doll and I'll go," he offered. "I won't even shoot you."

"The doll isn't important." Deidre controlled her rasping breath with an effort. "It's what's inside." She smiled in a deprecatory way. "A million in Bling-blings."

The little man's eyes went wide and white, as he jerked up with a start. "You know 'bout them?"

"I know lots of things, Mr. Steiner."

"Nobody's s'posed to know 'bout the Bling-blings, Bitch!" Then he tossed a look over one shoulder. "I'm tryin' to work, here, Leon. If you don't stop jaw-flappin' 'bout things you ain't s'posed to jaw-flap, I'm gonna' blow your balls off!"

Deidre's eyebrows raised, but her voice went flat. "You planned to steal the doll from the beginning, didn't you?"

"Jesus!" he whispered, backpedaling a step. He looked stupid, his eyes glazed. "You're hooked into the CIA's brain-drain machine."

Renewed confidence, as a result of his utterance, prompted the blind woman to lift her chin boldly. "Lock, stock and barrel," she lied.

"You can't do that!" He waggled a threatening finger. "I know my fuckin' rights. Nobody can scan my brain without a fuckin' warrant. And ain't no warrant here."

"The CIA doesn't need warrants." She smiled, coolly, again. "I'm going to drain your brain, Mr. Steiner."

"You don't know who you're fuckin' with, Bitch!" He tossed a worried look over his right shoulder. "Tell her, Leon. Tell her who she's fuckin' with."

"By the time I'm done, Mr. Steiner, what few brains you have will look like dessert sand."

"I'm warnin' you, Bitch. You're fuckin' over Plan 'A'!" Again he glanced around. "Tell her she's fuckin' over Plan 'A', Leon." He glared back at Deidre. "Nobody, but nobody, fucks over Plan 'A'."

"I don't care about your plans, Mr. Steiner. All I care about is hanging onto a million in Bling-blings."

"They're mine."

"Nonsense. I have them so they're mine. Why don't you save what's left between your ears, and go home?"

"I'm captain a' the ship!" Steiner's face twisted with rage as he thumped his narrow chest. "I give the orders!" He took a threatening step toward her. "I order you to give me the doll!"

"Mr. Steiner, you're a lunatic up a creek without a paddle." Another smile. "How's your draining brain feeling? A little pain? Ringing in your ears? A new voice telling you to go home?"

The little man thrust the flashlight at her, his free hand rising to clutch at the foil. "Stop fuckin' with me, Bitch!"

"Come, now, Mr. Steiner. Surely you've had bigger problems than a blind woman messing with your head? What about descriptions by family, teachers and friends? Or being arrested by the police followed by an orifice probing? When was the last time you talked with you P-Doc? Did you kill your therapist like you killed Meri Darling?"

"Bitch, you're pissin' me off." He glanced around. "Tell her what happens to bitches who piss me off, Leon."

"Mr. Steiner, I'm not even warmed up." She gave a tiny shrug. "When was the last time you looked in the mirror? Now, that must be an absolute eye-watering piss-off. Or how about your long-standing condemnations by religious advisors and therapists. Talk about pisserooni." Her voice dropped to a tauntingly confidential tone. "Not to mention all those angry bites from kittens and puppies. Poor Mr. Steiner. It must be terrible to be universally hated."

"There's no bigger piss-off, Bitch, than a drained brain and a fucked Plan 'A'!" He continued to stroke the foil as if his head ached. "My batteries are dead."

"That hardly comes as a shock."

"According to Nietzsche, 'There are no facts, only interpretations.'" The little man glared at Deidre his jaw muscles flexing. "Which means, Bitch, I'm tired of interpretin' your fuckin' facts for my fuckin' facts, when your fuckin' facts are fuckin' over my fuckin' facts." Steiner joggled the flashlight, as his free hand dropped and then went akimbo at his hips. "You know what that means, Bitch?"

Deidre raised her eyebrows. "Dare I assume Plan 'B'?"

Steiner's arms went up and down like the wings of a flapping duck trying to rise from a tar pit. In so doing, the flashlight beam blazed in all directions.

"How can we go to fuckin' Plan 'B' when there ain't no fuckin' Plan 'B'?" Steiner rubbernecked. "Tell her how it's all her fault because she fucked up Plan 'A', Leon!"

The little man's confused frustration brought out amusement at the corners of Deidre's mouth. "If I'm not being too presumptuous, Mr. Steiner, have you considered remedial therapy? I'll be happy to write a recommendation."

"I was therapized up the ass, Bitch!"

"What was the latest recommendation? Indeterminate incarceration?"

"No, Bitch! Some lyin' bastard called me a homicidal maniac and locked me up for life. Like I'm a common criminal." He let go a whimper. "Not even birthdays out to dip my wick."

"Why did you kill Meri Darling?"

"That fuckin' cunt crossed me." He reached up and replaced the foil cap's batteries. The blinking lights danced a kaleidoscope of colors across the darkened room, as he let the expired batteries drop to the floor. "We had a deal. We'd made plans. Then her and Sydney-Boy did an end run. Deidre, I haven't been able to sleep. My tummy hurts."

"I'm Mrs. Popovitch, to you."

"After you fucked up Plan 'A'? After I opened my fuckin' heart and soul to you? After all I've suffered because of you?" His eyes narrowed upon her. "Bitch, you're bleedin' me white!"

"Mr. Steiner, during our short but thoroughly disgusting association, I've come to the conclusion that any blood coming from you would be cold and green."

"You know… I hear that a lot." The little man's hands moved, bouncing the flashlight beam along the ceiling. "But, the truth is I'm just a guy gifted with unique brilliance." He rubbernecked. "Shut the fuck up, Leon! Everybody says I'm the one with the brains, not you!"

"Brains or not, Mr. Steiner, you're still a guy with no Plan 'B'."

The little man went over to the davenport, got down on his hands and knees, and peered underneath, using the flashlight to illuminate his visual search. Not finding anything beneath the furnishing, the little man stood, turned and strode back to the blind woman.

"According to Nietzsche: 'To live is to suffer, to survive is to find some meaning in the suffering.' And, Bitch, if you don't give me that fuckin'; doll I'm gonna' give you suffering like you've never had fuckin' suffering that suffers!"

Deidre grabbed her cane and rose to her feet. "In that case, Mr. Steiner, I'm going to do what you want."

"You are?" he gaped, taken completely by surprise.

"You've convinced me to cease my errant ways."

His eyes widened with hope. "You mean you'll be my whore?"

"No, Mr. Steiner. Instead, I've decided to give you the doll."

His face took on a disappointed look, and then brightened.

"A man of your unique brilliance deserves whatever he gets," Deidre continued.

The little man moved closer, his face scrunched with disbelief. "You're not just jerkin' my pud?"

"Trust me, Mr. Steiner, I wouldn't do that if you put a gun to my head."

He looked around grinning like a monkey sitting on a stack of bananas. "You hear that Leon? The Bitch is gonna' whip it to me." Then he looked back at her, squinting with curiosity. "My fuckin' personality, right? A little chit-chat from the Stein-Man and you're drippin' for it, right?"

"Puking over your sloth-like cunning would be closer to the mark. But, I'm sure the nausea will pass when I find my Dramamine."

Again, Steiner looked around the room. "You hear, Leon?" the little man shouted. "I scammed her with my sloth-like cunning. Bet you never did that."

"Why don't you have a seat, Mr. Steiner? Give your unbelievable brain a rest. And while you're letting sugar plums dance in your head, I'll go to the kitchen and get the doll."

"I could go with. We could get naked on the way back."

"As stomach-rolling as that sounds, I want to make this a surprise, something you'll take to your grave."

"I gotta' tell ya. My dick is jumpin'."

"If you're enjoying this, wait until you experience the finale." Deidre turned and tapped toward the kitchenette. "While you're waiting, hit the highpoints of your incredible career. I'm terribly interested."

"Bitch, you ain't heard nothin' 'til you've been high-pointed by me."

Steiner sidled over to the chair and sat down, gleeful over his unexpected change in fortune. "Where should I start?"

"Most biographies start at the beginning."

"You hear that Leon? We're talkin' book deal!"

"What are your early memories of family life, Mr. Steiner?" Deidre called, from the stove. She held a frying pan in one hand, hefting its weight. "Brothers? Sisters? What about your love life?"

"I never had no girlfriends 'cause I didn't have any sisters."

"I guess that's proof of God's mysteriously protective ways. Brothers?"

"I didn't have no brothers either except for Fat Tony. We were halfsies."

"Ah, so you came from a joined family. How interesting."

"I never joined nothing 'cause we never stayed anywhere very long. The cops were always on our asses."

"What did your father do to earn his living?"

The little man scratched his chin with the heel of one hand. "My old man was a booster."

"Every day must've been like Christmas with a criminal leading the Steiner clan."

"That depended on what he brung home. Car batteries ain't much fun. Unless you hook wires to the terminals and spark your balls."

"Sounds like you had a stimulating childhood."

She tapped back toward the rocker, keeping the pan concealed behind her skirt.

"What about your mother?" she asked.

"She was a whore."

"A professional woman. How nice."

"She's the reason I had lots of uncles."

"One can only imagine."

When Deidre reached the rocker she stopped, carefully concealing her violent intentions. "Now, I want you to hold out your hands and close your eyes, Mr. Steiner."

He glanced back growling, "Why the fuck should I?"

"Because I want to give you a big surprise."

"You hear that, Leon? I'm gonna' get surprised."

The blind woman reached out with her free hand to locate the little man's head. Upon doing so, she slid her fingertips over his face to make sure his eyes were closed.

"No peeking, Mr. Steiner," she instructed. "And hold still. This surprise is going to be an eye opener like you've never had."

A big grin spread across Steiner's face. "Bitch, ring my fuckin' chimes!"

Putting all her might behind the swing, Deidre struck out. There was a resounding ping as the steel cooking device bounced from Steiner's skull. The little man's scream of agony followed immediately. Stunned, he slumped out of the chair onto the floor.

"The Bitch killed me, Leon!"

Deidre dropped the pan and tapped her way as quickly as she could toward the cabin door.

"You're dead, Bitch!"

"Stay away!" she screamed.

"Get her, Leon!"

Steiner struggled to his feet then staggered after the blind woman.

Deidre reached the door and tried to turn the knob. It was locked.

Desperately, the blind woman fumbled with the latch but could not release it.

"Gotcha!" The little man grabbed Deidre by the hair.

With a cry of terror, Deidre twisted toward Steiner. She viciously raked his face with her fingernails, trying for his eyes.

Steiner staggered back cursing, rivulets of blood running down his cheeks.

Deidre stumbled away, her cane clicking on the floor.

Amidst a flurry of curses, Steiner rushed after her.

"I'm fuckin' gonna' beat your brains in like your brains ain't never been beat in before, Bitch!"

"Don't touch me!"

The little man slugged the side of her skull.

The blind woman dropped to the floor. She tried to get up, but he kicked her in the side. Her body coiled into a fetal position, the pain causing her to groan.

"Nietzsche said, 'There is more wisdom in your body than in your deepest philosophy.' Which means, Bitch, unless I get that doll it'll be time for me to learn all there is about your body."

"Wait!" she cried. One hand struck out protectively, swinging through air. "I gave the Bling-blings to Mr. Zeeman!"

"I told you, Bitch, he's dead."

"He's got them. They're in a pillow case," she explained, trying to rise.

"Sure you did, Bitch. Just like I couldn't smell your pussy as soon as I came in." He made an obscene popping noise with his mouth, and then kicked her back to the floor. "You, Bitch, are gonna beg me for it."

"Not if you provided the cyanide."

Deidre twisted her head back and forth, her ears focused upon Steiner's voice, trying to determine his exact position.

"You're lying to yourself, Bitch." Steiner smiled with his lower lip as his eyes veiled like a reptile's. "Tell her she's lying, Leon." He giggled hysterically. "Leon says you're lyin', too. You know what that means?"

"You're both maladjusted megalomaniacs."

"I'll bet your pussy tastes like salty caramel." He reached down, grabbed her hair, and dragged the blind woman to her knees. Then he tilted over her and licked one of her cheeks. "Salty as well as sweet." There was another moment of mad giggling. "You and me are fuckin' soul mates, Bitch."

"Search Mr. Zeeman's body. You'll find the Bling-blings."

Steiner gritted between his teeth, "As Nietzsche said, 'I'm not upset that you lied to me, I'm upset that from now on I can't believe you.' Tell the Bitch, Leon. Tell her how much her fuckin' lyin' makes me not believe her!"

"I'm not lying."

He knelt down next to Deidre, shoved her onto her back, grabbed her blouse and ripped the garment from her.

"No!" She again clawed at his face.

With a roar Steiner's swung at the blind woman. His fist caught her chin, banging Deidre's head against the floor, stunning her.

"Bitch, Bitch, Bitch." His eyes caressed the milky flesh swelling above her brassiere. "You could start your own dairy." Then he glanced to one side. "Stay back, Leon. This time, you're the one gettin' sloppy seconds."

"Charlie Owens is coming to drive me to the ferry. Look for yourself. My suitcases are by the door."

"Charlie Owens'll have to wait his turn. Right, Leon?" Steiner stood, his eyes still leering. "Bedtime, Bitch."

"No!" She tried to crawl away.

The little man reached down, grabbed her hair and jerked Deidre to her feet.

She quickly turned toward him. Then the blind woman lunged; her knee rising, catching Steiner sharply in the groin. Immediately, the little man dropped to his knees in squealing agony.

"Holy, fuckin' shit, Bitch! I think she busted my balls, Leon."

Deidre, having lost sense of where she was, staggered back toward the kitchen.

"According to Nietzsche," Steiner whimpered, 'it is impossible to suffer without making someone pay for it: every complaint already contains revenge.'" Steiner thrashed his way to his feet, his hands clawing at his aching groin. "Bitch, your ass is gonna' be my revenge!"

"If you touch me, I'll claw your eyes out!"

"Accordin' to my fuckin' P-Doc, nothin' pisses me off like rejection." Steiner gritted his ivories as he let go another shudder of pain. "I go shit-blind with rage. I lose control." He bent over at the waist, whining like a kicked puppy. "Sure, like everybody, I worry about vodka gettin' mixed with prune juice. Sure, like every purist, I get freaked out when I see pineapple on pizza." Finally, the little man forced himself upright. "But, ain't nothin' gets my hackles up worse than a balls-kickin' rejection!" He hobbled after her. "I'm gonna' cut out your eyes!"

Seconds later, Steiner caught up with Deidre.

"Let go!" The blind woman kicked out with her feet.

Steiner sharply jerked on the waistband of her slacks, sending the blind woman backward.

Unable to grab hold of something to break her fall, Deidre struck the floor with her head, leaving her skull bleeding and her insensible.

Steiner squatted down and quickly removed the rest of her clothing.

"Now that wasn't so bad, was it?" the little man mocked.

He let his eyes float across her flesh, enjoying the power he had over the blind woman's unmoving form. He delighted in the stirrings that her milky-white skin, taut breasts and walnut-size nipples created in his loins. His eyes scanned lower to dwell upon her slender waist, the slight swell of her hips, and the coil of dark hair between her legs.

"Nietzsche said, 'In every real man a child is hidden that wants to play.' And, Bitch, I intend to play until you fuckin' play me out."

Steiner changed position, kneeling next to Deidre's nakedness. With his hands, he fondled her breasts, weighing them, crushing them. Then, he bent over to suckle at her turgid nipples. While his mouth worked, the little man ran his right hand across her stomach and then into the triangle. Roughly, he forced two digits into her.

She moaned in pain; her eyes flickering open. Instinctively, Deidre batted at the point of intrusion.

Steiner sat upright, grinning as he watched her feeble efforts to force his hand away.

"I told you she'd love it, Leon."

"Please, stop!"

"Shut up, Bitch! You're fuckin' lovin' this."

"Please don't do this?"

"This is what's known as unvoluntary foreplay, Bitch. I play while you fuckin' unvolunteer." He cackled maniacally. "Ain't that right, Leon?"

Deidre twisted toward Steiner and lashed out with her feet. One bare heel caught Steiner's cheek, sprawling him backward. Naked, she scrambled to her feet and staggered off.

"I'm gonna' gut you from pussy to tits, Bitch! I'm gonna' kill you so dead you'll be the deadest dead you'll ever be, even before you're dead!"

Again he went after the blind woman.

In her hurried flight, Deidre toppled over a chair. The tumble winded her; the blind woman got to her knees; her breath gasping.

Steiner kicked Deidre onto her side. Then he unzipped his jeans and let them drop. His penis bloated with lust, pointed like a spear.

Deidre, sobbing, tried to rise.

The little man bent over and gave the back of her skull another stunning blow, plowing Deidre onto her side. Then, he kneeled over her still form and forced her face down.

Still vaguely conscious, the blind woman tried to rise.

"Hold her down, Leon!" the little man bellowed. "Quit squirmin', Bitch! You're spoiling my aim."

Steiner coiled a fist and put the weight of his entire body behind the next blow at her head.

Deidre went dead still.

A flash of rage crossed the little man's face then vanished. He reached out with both hands and jerked her legs apart. Quickly, he shifted his position so as to kneel between them.

"You've been begging for this, Bitch." He rubbed the head of his penis between the folds of her sex. "As Nietzsche said, 'The true man wants two things: danger and play. For that reason he wants woman, as the most dangerous plaything.' Personally, I'd prefer to fuck you dead."

He shoved inside her; his pelvic-thrust beast-like.

She whimpered in pain as his penis scored her vagina's dry walls. A gust of cold air crossed the room. In the distance, a siren wailed, rapidly coming closer.

"Tell me how you love it, Bitch!" Steiner giggled, his pelvis pounding against her buttocks. "Nietzsche says, 'We belong to a time in which culture is in danger of being destroyed by the means of culture.'" He gave his head a grinning shake, as his lust rose. "Which is why fuckin' you is the only way to save the whole fuckin' wo…"

Abruptly, his weight lifted from her; their bodies separating with distinct sucking noise.

Almost immediately, there was a muffled male scream, then a sharp snapping noise. This was followed by the sound of something heavy hitting the floor not far from where Deidre lay.

There was another gust of cold wind, through the cabin. Then stillness.

On the road outside the cabin, vehicle brakes squealed. Tires skidded on gravel. Car doors slammed. Then, came the sound of hurried footfalls through the snow toward the cabin door. That door opened with a bang, flooding the front room with icy air.

Deidre got to her hands and knees, bewildered and terrified.

The sound of heavy feet rushed across the cabin.

The blind woman struggled to her feet, staggering back, sobbing with fearful the expectancy.

"Mrs. Popovitch," Sheriff Sherman shouted. "This is the police."

"Help me," she cried. "A man raped me. He said he was going to kill me."

"You're safe, Mrs. Popovitch," Sherman returned. "Charlie Owens called us. He said two men were coming here. I see one on the floor next to an aluminum thing fitted with blinking lights. Where's the other?"

"There was only him. His name's Harry Steiner."

"Somebody get a blanket to cover her!" Sherman bellowed as he went over to where she was standing.

"He said he'd killed Meri Darling," Deidre continued. "He said he'd killed Mike Zeeman and Tio Menotti and my husband's father. He said he'd killed Mr. Kandinsky and poor Mr. Vasiliev. He said he was going to kill me."

Another officer rushed from the bedroom. He hurried over to the blind woman and draped a blanket around her naked form.

"I tried to fight him off," she sobbed, drawing the covering over her nakedness. "I kicked. I clawed, I hit him with a pan. I did all I could."

"Looks like you did enough," another voice said. "His neck's broke."

"I was trying to defend myself." Her words transformed to weeping.

"Calm down, Mrs. Popovitch," Sherman said, taking her hands in his. "Nobody's blaming you."

Chapter 16
"Resurrection"

Six months later, Deidre Popovitch was in the kitchen at Popovitch's Bed & Breakfast. Outside, the afternoon air was warm and breezy. Sea gulls screamed as they made hungry sweeps off the shoreline. Inside, in the kitchen, the blind woman kneaded dough. Her white cane rested against the counter not far from her work area. In the background, a radio played swing music. Above the bouncing music, she heard the front door open and close.

Deidre stopped her labors, grabbed the white stick and tapped into the reception room.

"I have only one cabin left," Deidre announced. "It's got twin beds." She quickly tapped to the reception desk. "Will that work for you?"

"I'm easy to please," Mike Zeeman returned.

The strange familiarity of his voice caused her to hesitate. "How many are you?"

"Just me."

"Vacations aren't as much fun alone."

"I'm in Hull on business."

She frowned, still trying to place his voice. Then, she sniffed. Even the scent of him held familiarity.

"How long will you be staying?" Deidre asked.

"Just tonight."

The blind woman settled into the chair behind the desk. "Short stay."

"I owe somebody money."

"That makes you a novelty. Most people are looking for what's owed them."

"I'd have paid it sooner. But I had trouble collecting on a contract. Doing that caused complications."

"Sounds exciting."

"You and your husband run this place?"

"I'm divorced."

"I'm sorry to hear that."

"Don't be. I got this place as part of my divorce settlement." Her beautiful face relaxed in a rueful smile. "I met this man who apologized all the time. He's dead, now." She sniffed. "God, you smell good." She felt across the desk for the registration book. "You'll have to forgive me. I spend so much time alone. I forget that people have things to do other than chit-chat." When she located the book, Deidre pushed it toward him. "Please sign in."

"It's Mike Zeeman, Deidre."

Her heart heaved in her chest. Her mouth dropped open. She rose to her feet on trembling legs.

"You're dead!" she gasped.

"Not just yet."

"But, Mr. Steiner said he'd killed you."

He raised his eyebrows. "Steiner tried."

"After the police found Mr. Menotti's body in the ocean, everybody just assumed that yours had been put in there."

"The bullet creased my skull instead of going through."

"Are you, uh, on the glam?"

"The phrase is, 'on the lam.' And no. After settling things in Boston I took some time to think about who I had become and where I was headed. I didn't like myself or my prospects. So, I spent some time wandering around, making amends—I guess you could say I repaired a whole lot of burnt bridges. You're my last stop on this journey."

"Me?"

He hesitated, smiling. "I stopped at 5 Derne Street. The Russian said you'd moved to Hull. Serge Vasiliev is getting around pretty, good. A man his age usually doesn't make a comeback after such a close call."

"He's marrying Dasha next week."

Deidre stretched out one hand and came around the desk, staggering as if she might fall.

Zeeman rushed over and caught her by the shoulders.

Instantly, her hands went to his face and her fingers danced across his skin. After a few seconds she let go a sigh.

"I had to be sure," she murmured. "I had to know that I wasn't hallucinating."

"Your share of the Bling-blings is nearly six hundred thousand."

"My share?" She staggered a step back in shock. "You mean you're here to pay me?"

"It's a cashier's check. I can drive you to the bank."

Her arms rose and fell. "That's impossible."

"You still think I'm dead?"

"A man actually kept faith with me!"

"To be honest, it was a close call."

"The police say I killed Steiner. I don't know how I broke his neck. I guess when I kicked out at him. He was... he..."

"You didn't kill him, Deidre."

"But I did. I even got a reward for his capture." She nibbled her lip. "I can't tell you the number of people who've stopped in just to shake my hand for a murder well done."

"Deidre, I killed him."

She blinked several times in surprise. "You?"

"After Steiner shot me, I was unconscious for a while. When I woke up, I heard you screaming. I went into your cabin. And that was that."

The blind woman made her way back to the chair and sat down. She remained silent, wiping the wet trickling from her eyes.

"What's wrong?" he asked.

"I don't know whether to be happy for me, or sad for you."

"The Russian said to tell you how much you're missed."

Her free hand rose and fell. "I wouldn't be speaking about Mr. Vasiliev if he wasn't marrying Dasha."

"I thought you liked the old fellow."

"That was before I discovered he was a nudist."

Zeeman blinked in confusion. "Deidre, lots of people are nudists. And considering that you're..."

"Nudity, for a blind woman, isn't a problem," she cut in. "But, he was stark naked during all my Russian lessons." Her shoulders lifted and fell. "The least he could've done was tell me."

"I suppose he didn't think it mattered." Then Zeeman frowned. "How did you know he was naked?"

"It was during my last lesson. We stopped for a snack. Serge was serving a Russian version of pigs in a blanket." One hand dragged a lock of hair away from her forehead. "I reached out for a second portion and grabbed something entirely different."

He laughed.

She let go a long sigh. "What his whatchamacallit was doing on the table, next to the serving plate, I can only imagine."

"I take it you dropped your handful?"

Her cheeks pinked, slightly as her smile broadened. "Eventually."

The tall man reached into his suit and withdrew a banker's envelope. He placed it on the edge of the desk against one of her hands.

She clutched the paper wrapper and reached out with the other hand, fumbled for a moment before locating her cane.

"I know it doesn't make up for what I put you through," he told her.

"Nonsense." She got to her feet. "Verbal jousting with you was the best time I'd had since marrying Sydney."

"Then, I'm forgiven?"

The blind woman clattered around the desk to him and slid her free arm around his neck. Then, she kissed him.

Zeeman pulled Deidre tightly to him. A soft moan escaped her.

"How long can you stay?" she murmured into his ear.

He sniffed. "I smell something burning."

"Damn!"

She retreated from his embrace and tapped back into the kitchen. "I forgot about my popovers. Promise you'll stay for more than one night? There's so much I want to talk about."

"I'll stay as long as you want."

Zeeman followed her as far as the kitchen doorway. He watched Deidre drop the envelope into a pile of flour, fumble for baking mitts, open the oven, bend over and remove a pan of toasty brown puffs.

"What do you think?" She set the pan on the stove top.

"Everything's perfect."

Books by Michael Paulson

Blind Woman's Bluff
Cherem
Dead On*
Deadly Age*
Deadly Sting*
Deadly Trade*
Deadly Turn*
I, Philibert Q. Winslow
The Van Gogh Deception
Who Killed Michael Douglas

*Deacon Bishop Detective series

www.ingramcontent.com/pod-product-compliance
Lightning Source LLC
Chambersburg PA
CBHW070035260626
47159CB00005B/2047